A LEGEND FOR THE NEW MILLENNIUM AND BEYOND.

*"The challenge may not be in seeing what lies ahead,
but in recognizing what we left behind."*

*Dedicated to my mom & dad in honor of their fiftieth
wedding anniversary. They gave me the ability to know
right from wrong and the courage to act on it.*

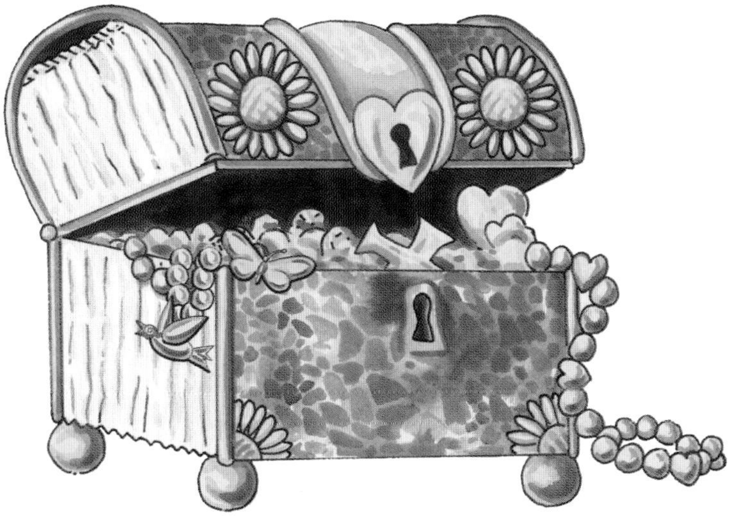

Jewel Box & Friends

Andover, Kansas

Published in the United States by Jewel Box & Friends, 324 Lakecrest Drive, Andover, Kansas 67002. Manufactured in the United States.

Cataloging-in-Publication Data:
Library of Congress Catalog Card Number: 99-90515
ISBN 0-9672202-0-3

Printed in the United States
First Edition

Jacket design by Larry Stephenson. All rights reserved. Copyright 1999
Layout: Larry Stephenson with help from Randy Stephenson
Original verse: Larry Stephenson pages 1- 39.
Closing verse: Patti Weinbrenner page 41
Editors: Sarah L. Riehm & Naomi Phinney

A word of thanks.

This book never would have become a reality without the help of a few close friends. I wish to thank Tom and Martha Marple, for encouraging me to write the book. The king and queen are named in their honor. No parallels should be drawn between the characters. Tom is the most unselfish man I have ever known. Martha is his strength.

It may be unusual in such a busy age for three siblings to collaborate on a book such as this. I wish to thank my younger brother, Randy, for helping me design the layout. My sister, Patti Weinbrenner, undertook the job of adding the spit and polish while refining the final product. She also is instrumental in marketing the book. I thank Patti for coauthoring the story in its final edit. Her unselfish efforts made this book possible.

No book can ever be born without the aid of an insightful and encouraging editor. I had two of them. Thank you, Sarah and Naomi.

And most of all, I thank my best friend and wife, Sheryl, for supporting me in so many ways. We have worked as partners for more than a quarter century. Together, we toast the beginning of the next Millennium.

The Butterfly King

Written & Illustrated by

Larry Stephenson

Coauthored by

Patti Weinbrenner

Somewhere in the far distant universe beyond the limitations of imagination, the year was 1999 Millennian time. This is not to be confused with times on earth, for history has been known to repeat itself many times throughout the galaxies. From the beginning, Millennians turned their eyes skyward with curiosity. The heavens were considered to be the gardens of the gods. A Master Juggler held the Universe in orbit while constantly rotating planets around a Sun. On the night our story begins, with a simple twist of his hand, the Master Juggler spun a small jewel of a planet into perfect motion at the far corner of the galaxy. Like a spinning top, Earth, as it came to be known, began its journey into our story's time.

I was comrade, confidante, and entrusted scribe. My official duty was to record the King's legacy, but I was also an appointed Friend of the King. The King acquired his friends by either appointing or buying them. He selected only the finest friends - the prosperous, the dashing, the brilliant or the comic. As a member of this special brotherhood, it was my responsibility to set history straight. I was the lover of legends, a teller of tall tales. I was the Court Scribe. Moreover, I was the King's true friend. Thomas Maximus trusted me with writing his story into *The Legend of Fables and Myths*, lest it too be lost like history before it.

The King was born into royalty and wealth - a legend in waiting. He was destined to become the monarch, and the throne was conferred to Thomas on his eleventh birthday. Carefully chosen courtiers helped Thomas grow as a scholar, a soldier, and a man of fashion. Dangerously handsome, the King had his choice of any maiden in the kingdom. He chose Martha - a fortunate selection. Not only was she beautiful, but she proved to be equally intelligent and witty.

Over the years, Thomas appeared to weather well. An air of aged experience replaced his dashing good looks. If only what seemed to be was so! I knew Thomas as a small child - before he took the throne. From the moment Thomas Max first put on the rose-colored glasses of his station, his perspective began to distort. Fool or respected King; that was yet to be decided!

"Shazam, Kabam, I'm the Magic Man!" the wizard exhaled into the cool night air. An eerie mist escaping from the nearby lake settled around his feet. Thomas Maximus, King of Hearts, stood close by petting his dog with one hand as he brushed away fog with the other. We often traveled out onto the moor to escape the village lights and study the heavens. It was there at the edge of the bog, on this last night of winter, that Earth was seen for the very first time.

Rhubarb, the dog trainer, stood dutifully by our sides as he always did on these nightly

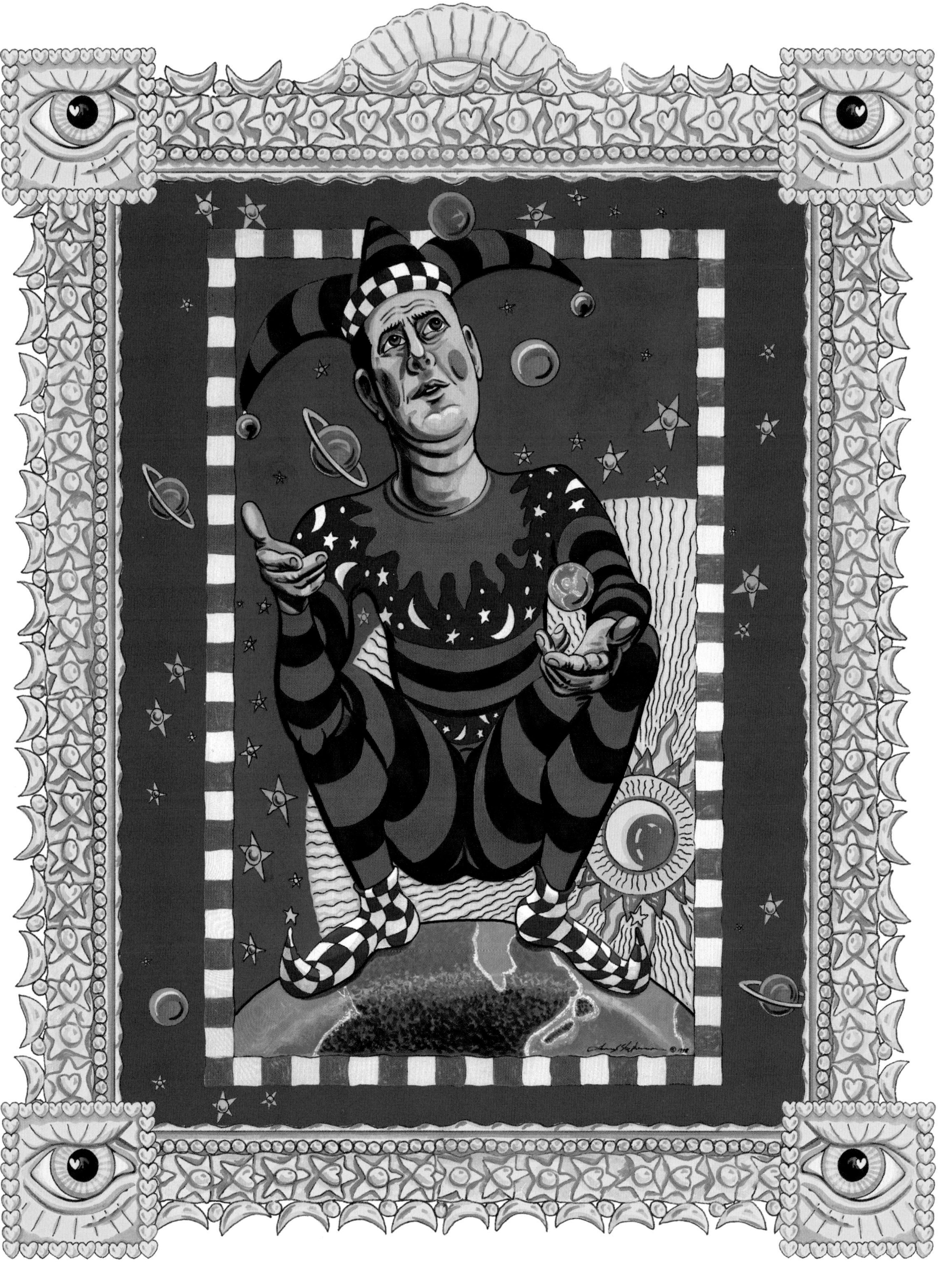

excursions. The youngest of the crew, he too was considered one of the brotherhood even though he had no great wealth, wit or wisdom. Rhubarb was yet to turn sixteen. The King had enlisted Rhubarb to lead his prize dog, Baby, on this pilgrimage onto the moor. Wild boars with razor tusks roamed the bogs late at night. Koodoos - the nastiest, ugliest, foulest-smelling carnivores - frequented the banks of the lake on the other side. We had crossed the imaginary line to the distant shore leaving common sense behind. There was good reason to worry. Danger was all around us. The dog stood guard.

This newest astrological find electrified us all. The Master Juggler had just tossed up another planet - unusual for this time of year. This could be an omen. Quickly scrambling out of the bog onto the King's Highway, we rushed toward the safety of the village. We knew that Koodoos were reluctant to roam into town.

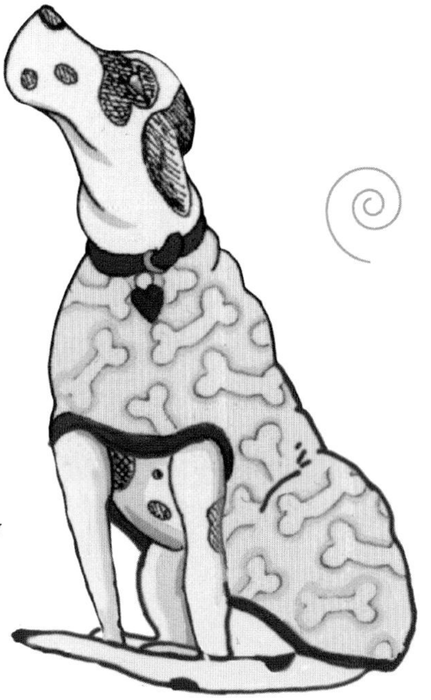

"Shazam, Kabam, I'm the Magic Man," the wizard gleefully sang into the brisk darkness.

"Yahoo and whoop-de-doo, I am King and never are you!" the King retorted. The remark disappointed us all, but we had come to accept Thomas's more selfish moments.

"Boo-hoo, dippity-doo, I am the dog of you know who," Baby howled back to the moon in perfect accompaniment. Even she was excited. New planets were not born just any day!

Wizz may have made the discovery, but I must confess he knew little about magic. He was, however, the King's closest ally and one of my finest friends. Cast by the King, Wizz had agreeably played the part. Like the rest of us, he was an appointed friend who accepted the expectations of the brotherhood. Playing with magic was entertaining. And from the time Wizz first connected the motions of the heavens with the changing of day into night, he had become fascinated with astronomy. Wizz was a bony creature. High cheekbones and a bulbous nose punctuated his pinched face. The pointed hat on his head studded with stars and moons mirrored the conical shape of his long flowing beard. As old as the hills, the wizard's twisted fingers spoke volumes.

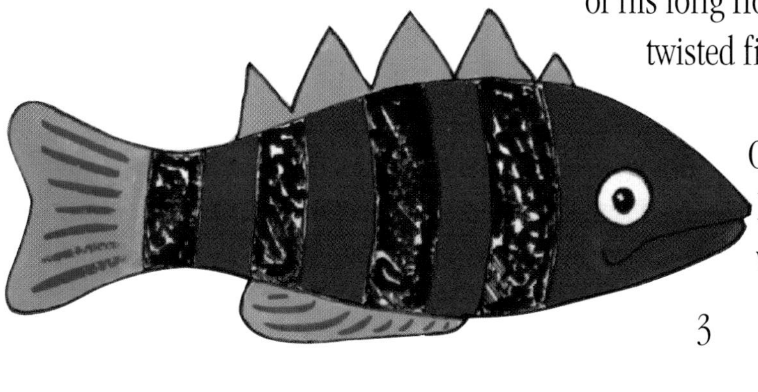

Our dog handler, brother, and fellow stargazer, Rhubarb loved these country outings. Rhubarb worshiped clean air, cherished virgin waters, and respected everything that could walk, swim or fly. Love radiated from Rhubarb the way heat blazed from the sun. He glowed from his carrot-top hair down to his size thirteen shoes. Tall and lanky, Rhubarb stretched across a six-foot-four-inch frame that refused to keep up when he walked. He was often seen gliding through the village streets head and shoulders above the crowd while engrossed in a book. As if he were in a trance, Rhubarb floated through life. On the occasions when he did touch the ground, he always landed on his feet.

Although she was not his own, Rhubarb loved his canine charge. She was a big, hairy leaner with a log for a tail. A black and white Harlequin Dane, Baby was the King's dog and closest friend. She was indeed the Queen's only competition for the King's affections.

We made up rhymes while skipping home. Bubbling over with enthusiasm, our voices pierced the night air:

A pig on wing is a curious thing.
It takes the farmer to make them sing.
Give a pretty gold coin to see them fly.
If swine can grow feathers, then so can I!"

"Boo-hoo," howled the dog.

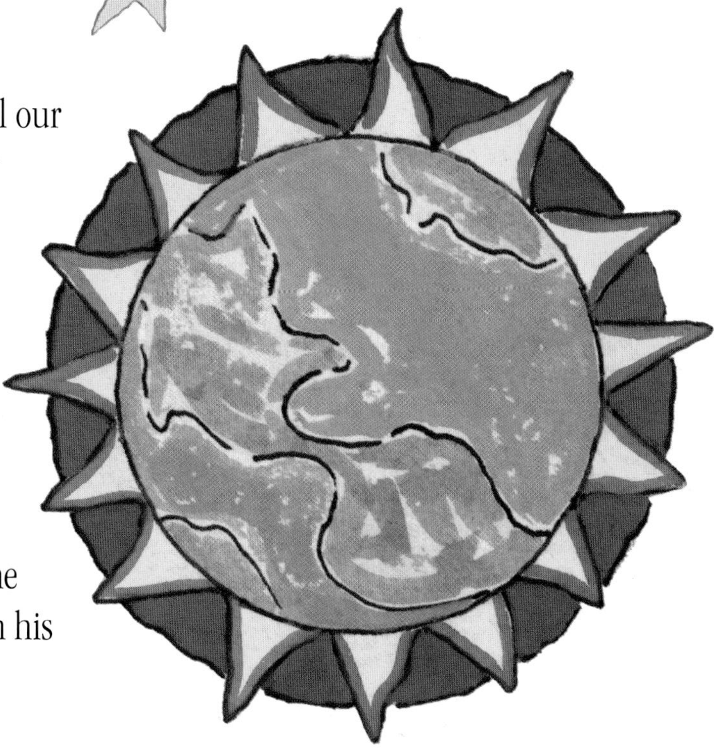

That night, we sang into the heavens until our voices departed us. The King believed our discovery would make him immortal. Arriving back at the castle, the King dismissed us until the following morning when he would require a few friends for tea. Wizz and the King retired to the map room to chart the new planet.

"What does it mean my wizard friend?" the King inquired as Wizz refined the point on his goose quill pen.

"Signs such as this one often mean impending doom. When a new planet is born, an older planet must die. Only so much space in the Universe, my enlightened King," Wizz prophesied.

"Gobbledygook! I refuse to listen to such idle chatter," the King retorted. He preferred to think he would remain immortal. The coming of the end of Mill is not what he desired to hear.

"Perhaps the coming of a new age," the wizard said reversing his reply.

This pleased Thomas, and he retired for the evening leaving Wizz to chart the new planet and draw his map.

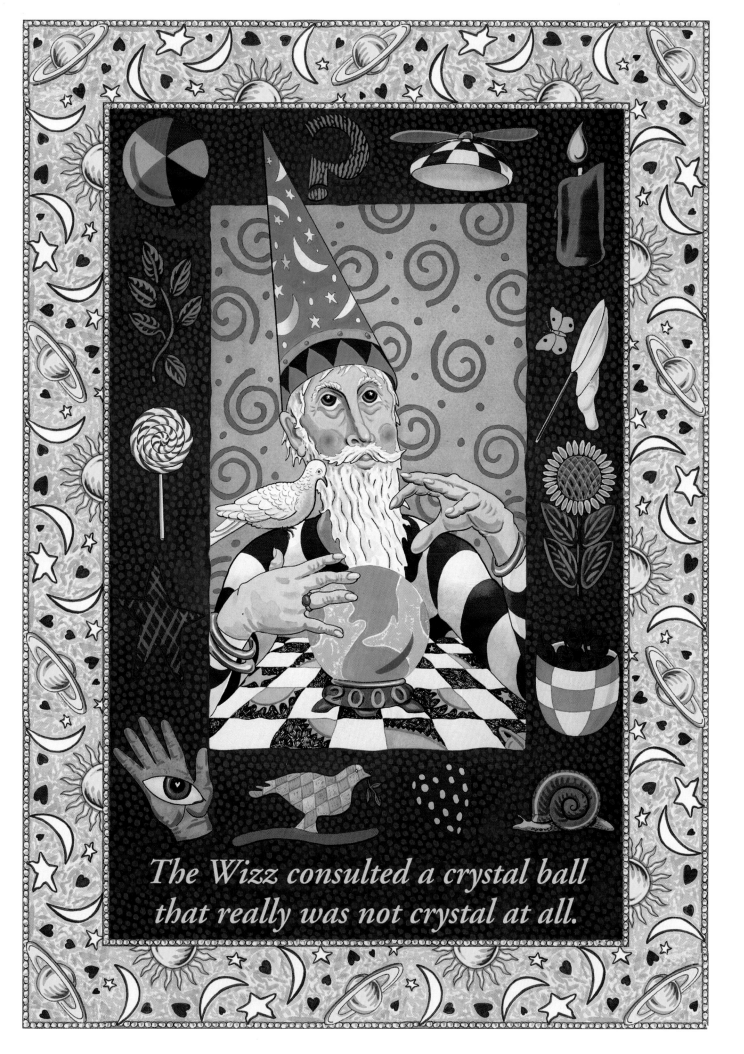

The Wizz consulted a crystal ball
that really was not crystal at all.

As morning retreated, the King awoke and climbed the tower steps. The second moon was setting in the southern sky as the King watched for his Queen. A hundred archers stood guard on the castle walls while patrolling for koodoos. Martha was visiting the neighboring countryside and gathering morels from the nearby woods. The King could view the entire kingdom from his crow's nest above the palace. There slept Wizz draped over the map table. The quill had dropped to the stone floor beneath his feet. The makings of the map served as his pillow. Thomas Max walked to the edge of an open window and surveyed the kingdom of Mill, as a gray mist permeated the outside air dotted with gliding butterflies.

The rumble of thunder rolled across the planted plains surrounding the palace walls. The King could smell the perfume of spring pear blossoms hanging in the muggy dampness as storm clouds gathered in the distance. The coming storm reflected off a face that resembled a book marked by countless years of ruling the tiny kingdom of Mill. Each line and crevice told a story. His green eyes twinkled behind the rose-colored glasses.

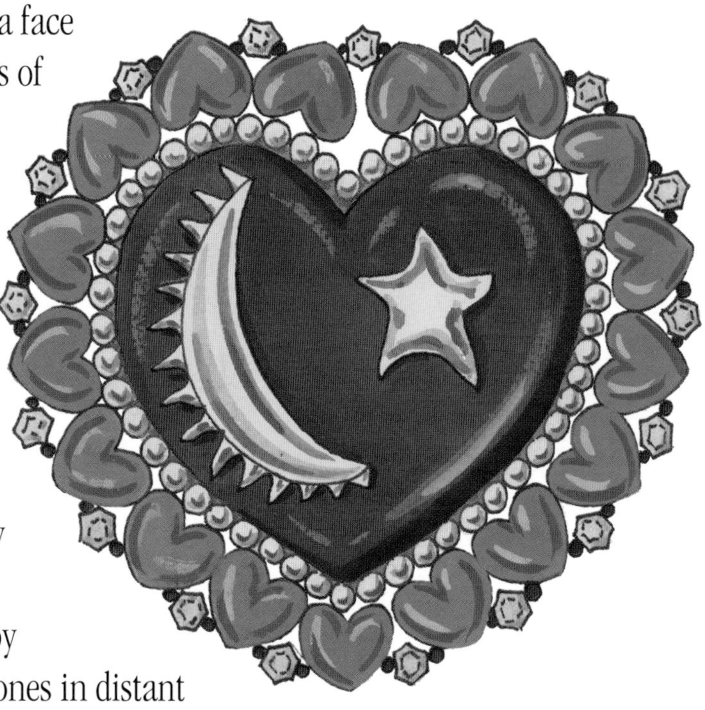

Thomas Maximus, King of Hearts - his title suited him to a fare-thee-well. Pinned squarely to his chest was the heart to prove it. No one wore a grander heart than the jewel hanging on his own breast, surrounded in heavy gold, hand-shaped by the finest craftsmen and embellished with smaller lapis hearts bordered by emeralds and rubies. Widgins had mined the stones in distant lands long since forgotten. This jewel-encrusted valentine symbolized the goodness he desired. Thomas Max wanted to be a good King. Not necessarily great, he would settle for just good-of-heart if he only could. He desired that all his subjects follow his example. Thus, the wearing of hearts came into fashion.

All the people of Mill wore hearts sewn to the outsides of their garments. Yet, they were empty inside. No one in the land possessed a real heart or knew the difference. They were proud of an outward display. Still, no one could claim a heart as significant as the King. Thomas had seen to that. Over the years, some of the sewn-on hearts became larger as bigger became better. This pleased the King. It was valuable to be able to identify people by the size of their hearts.

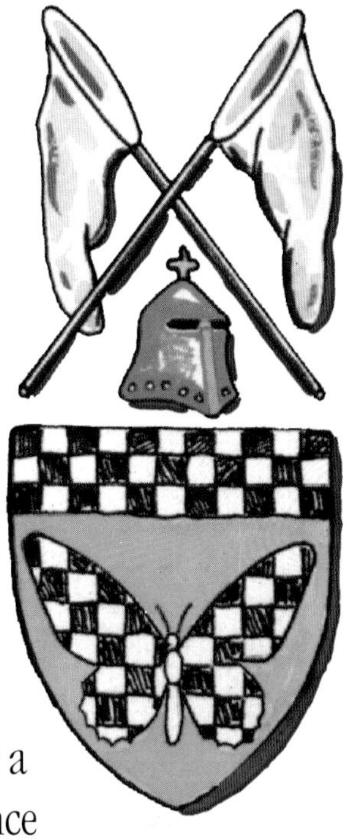

Designers of the day kept the court in vogue with their seasonal lines of fashionable, fabric hearts. Being good-hearted was as simple as sewing on the proper heart. Doing good came into style, and some people became known as do-gooders. Mimicking their King, these do-gooders refused to acknowledge evil or disappointment. But none knew the satisfaction that came to life with a physical beating heart.

I had climbed the stairs to the palace tower. Wizz still slept at his map room table. The King slowly sipped tea while watching butterflies catch the updrafts that surrounded the tower walls.

As he leaned on the stone ledge of the arched opening, Thomas looked out over a panorama of rolling countryside. Royal knights chased butterflies in the distance while wasting another day into the next. No one knew why. Or cared. Like Thomas, the knights had long since lost any purpose in life. Chasing butterflies was all that seemed important. Storm clouds were on the horizon, and Thomas mused that his knights had best stop before they got all wet. What curious behavior I thought...not a single knight knew when to come in out of the rain. These things never fretted the King. He could see nothing dire through the rose-colored glasses now permanently affixed to his face. For many years, the King had refused to remove them from his nose. He had long since forgotten how. The Knights continued at play as the sky blackened around them.

The fragrance of the coming rain chased an approaching silhouette. It appeared at first to be only a gray speck on the distant horizon. As it grew larger the King recognized it as a vehicle of the court. A large jeweled crown was attached to its roof. The entire carriage was clearly marked with the royal checkerboard. Wheels were reminiscent of large sunflowers with hubs like spinning butterflies. Synchronized white horses puffed steam as they raced to escape the building storm.

"Open the gates," bellowed the King at the top of his lungs. The team of horses roared up the road and onto the bridge. Their pounding hooves battered the oak planks while crossing the trestle as they entered the palace walls.

The building shook. Wizz stirred at his post. Damp drool tattooed the map table where the wizard's face had been at rest. "Shazam, Kabam," Wizz mumbled and fell back into his dreams.

The Queen's chariot raced to a halt below the King's open portal. Martha had been the fairest maiden in all the land. Her skin was white as the powder atop Mill's mountain peaks and pure like the rivers, which flowed from the summits. Her auburn braids were now seasoned into salt and peppered locks. The scent of crushed rose petals had been replaced by the smell of lilac.

At that very moment a cloud split, lightning crashed and rain burst through the open window. Wizz awoke with a shudder! Moisture dripping down his large nose formed a puddle on the table beside him. It seemed to me that at first he thought it was from the passing rain. Baby's second lick soon changed his mind. She was at home on any piece of furniture in the palace. It had taken Baby little effort to scale the map table to position herself at the window beside her King. Wizz dodged an oncoming lick as Baby thumped her tail and jarred the table. She

was half the size of a horse and shed a trail of black and white hair wherever she went.

"Get off that table!" the Queen barked as she rushed into the room. Martha did not allow animals on the furniture. Baby quickly sank to the floor seeking a place to hide. Stern as steel, Martha was not to be messed with. "A sign appeared in the sky last evening," she stated. "Some say it is a message from a god."

It was my sworn duty to observe the facts and record them accordingly. I was amazed! How did she know? Where did she hear? Word traveled fast in the kingdom of Mill. I later learned that

9

Rhubarb had told the gardener about our discovery only that morning as he walked the dog.

"The Master Juggler tossed up a new planet," Martha went on, "and the countryside is awash in speculation."

The King turned to face his wizard who was now fully awake and looking for his map. "Some wise words for your King?" asked Thomas.

The wizard worked frantically to smooth out his map that had been torn into small pieces by the dog. He had charted the planet before he fell asleep. With no answer imminent, the Queen quickly vacated the room with a look of disgust painted across her face. The King was at her heels. A thumping echoed as the dog followed them through the open exit.

"An omen of great things to come," shouted Wizz.

"What a bore," whispered the Queen. I guessed that Martha disapproved of Thomas's band of rogues. I sometimes felt that she did not care for the brotherhood we all shared.

That afternoon I stood in the tower as the wizard modeled a sphere painted to resemble the new planet he had discovered. He redrew his map and named the planet Earth. As he gazed into the new globe, I believe he imagined that he could see into the future, "Shazam, Kabam, I'm a Magic Man." Deliriously happy, Wizz danced a jig as he held up his ball. He clicked his heels and waltzed around the room with his precious planet cradled in his arms. Common sense had escaped him as it had his King. This foolishness was becoming infectious.

Days passed before the wizard reported again to his King. When he spoke, he lectured scientifically, "The arrival of a new planet is indeed an uncommon occurrence. Perhaps it is a sign of the turning of time. The year 2000 is approaching. I believe this is a proclamation glowing in the heavens." Wizz stared into his sphere and convinced Thomas Max that this was an event of historical proportions. "A party should be planned. The Queen should be consulted," Wizz suggested. Martha was widely respected for her spectacular parties, plus Wizz needed to score some points with the Queen. I kept copious notes of all these discussions. History was being recorded.

When the King met with his Queen, she had a brilliant suggestion, "The King should name a party Millennium in honor of the people of Mill." The Queen recognized the opportunity for her King to shine. It was, after all, the turning of time. A second thousand years in the making called for a special occasion. And so, we called it a Millennium in honor of the King's subjects.

As part of the celebration, Thomas Max decided to announce a special butterfly-chasing contest. With little else to occupy time, wellborn Millennians loved to play. Games such as playing favorites and jumping through hoops were considered Royal Games. The favorite sport of the land was Chasing Butterflies. This often required catching the creatures in nets, while riding backwards on horseback. The King's knights were very good at Chasing Butterflies. They had done so throughout the centuries refining the skill from one generation to the next. Soon, Chasing Butterflies became the national pastime of the land of Mill. For the Millennium extravaganza, all would be invited to participate - not just the royals.

For added festivities, the King spoke of jugglers juggling, jesters joking, and musicians making melodies. Everyone would be at play, as the nation chased butterflies into the next Millennium. A dance would be held, and a huge fair would cover the grounds below the castle walls. With the Queen's assistance, this would be a festival to remember!

The next day the Queen began organizing in earnest. She called in her most worldly advisers. "To fit the kingdom in its party clothes, first, it must be measured," observed the Queen. Tape Measurers were employed to survey every building, fountain, and architectural feature from top to bottom. Custom-crafted banners were then fitted by the finest tailors to hang from every structure. As each detail was completed, it led to another idea.

"Bakeoffs must be held to find the perfect pastries," suggested the Queen. Two thousand Food Tasters followed a thousand Bakers. "The finest designers will dress the Court," the Queen commanded. A parade of lace-covered garments was followed by a selection of eatable accessories to consume at the banquet.

Twaddle and balderdash! The unthinkable was about to occur. This might be the gala to end all galas. It would not be just any ho-hum commemoration! Even though history repeated itself every few thousand years or so, this called for a grand shindig. It would be greater than history should ever allow or might want to allow ever again! A nonsensical virus had begun to spread.

The King continued to consult his wizard. But in his sphere, Wizz saw life on Mill exactly as his King presumed it should be. His appointed job was to always tell the King exactly what he wanted to hear.

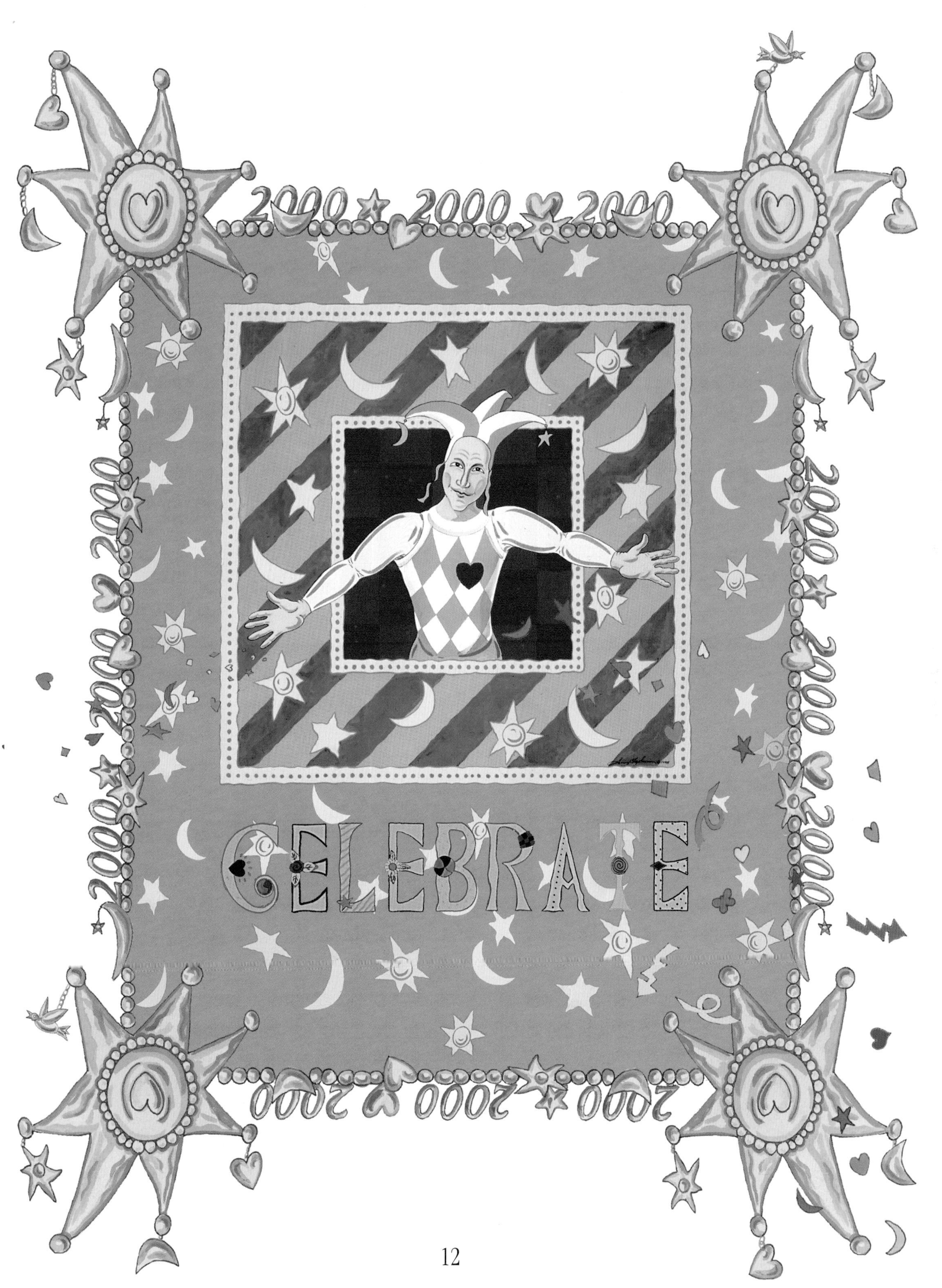
2000 2000 2000
CELEBRATE
2000 2000 2000

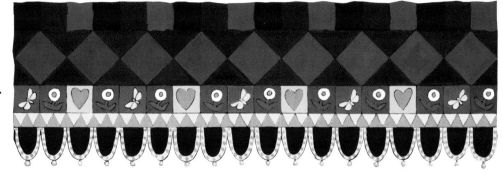

This pleased the King, who lived in a world unto himself behind his rose-colored glasses. Each day appeared to Thomas Max as an overflowing bowl of cherries or an all-day sucker. Suckers and cherries were things that the King cherished most. The King had a huge appetite for daydreaming, and Wizz reinforced the King's dreams by seeing them in the globe. In the King's mind some days passed as slowly as snails. When he wished it, other days disappeared with the snap of a finger. The Queen disapproved of such silliness, but she could not control her King nor the folly of the Court. Senselessness abounded in the land of Mill.

*A*n assortment of oddballs combined to form the King's Court. There were few among us with the common sense of a stone. Its fashionable members were a mixture of royalty, artists, and fools. An official fool dressed the part, but the biggest fools were never so clearly defined. The King enjoyed surrounding himself with the most creative people. Conical hats and flowing robes tailored from richly colored fabrics adorned the aristocracy of the land. Fools and jesters wore hats with triple cones decorated with bells and whistles. Peasants, country gentlemen, serfs, and farmers dressed in less formal attire. Those connected to the arts embellished their bodies to total perfection. Rings covered every finger, every toe. Tattoos to kazoos were painted or attached to every limb and facial feature.

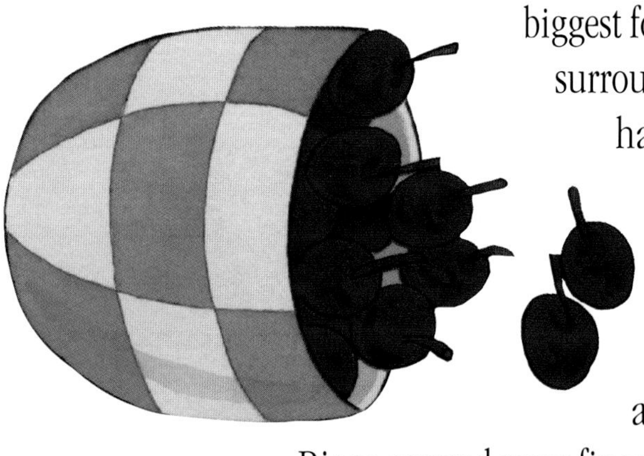

"Artsy, smartsy whoop-de-doo, I'm not crazy but so are you," was the sanctioned cheer. Nothing was beginning to make sense. The King's Court was on a lark.

Each passing day the clock seemed to gain speed. The party date was rapidly approaching, and the Queen was showing the first cracks of stress. Martha personally supervised even

13

the smallest detail. It had been little more than a month since the Millennium had been announced, but already knights practiced their horsemanship and polished the handles on their finest nets. Jesters were trying out jokes and jugglers feverishly prepared tricks. The best bakers baked and the most creative cake decorators created. The Queen was busy juggling her committee of experts. They practiced eating pastries with silver spoons. Some ate too well and became obese - a marvelous sight to Thomas Max through his rose-colored glasses. Music filled the air as the Queen held auditions for the perfect dance band. Actors and puppeteers rehearsed inside brightly colored booths designed for the upcoming fair. Dancers danced in the Village Square, and artists created long flowing banners - embellished with braids and tassels - that hung from palace walls and fluttered over the Cobblestone Square. The excitement was contagious.

The Queen described to me a birthday cake for the Millennium covered in icing loaded with fresh forest nuts, wild berries and cherry liqueur folded into heavy cream. This would top several sheets of soft, dark chocolate modeled over multiple layers of rich, chocolate cake sandwiched between cream filling brimming with cherries and berries. The cake would stretch from one floor to the next. The construction of such a cake would be a feat unto itself. On top of the cake would sit four custom candles sculpted to form 2000. In the Queen's dreams, it would take an elevator simply to reach the upper layers of the cake. An architect soon was added to the Queen's subcommittee on cakes.

The wizard stood in the crow's nest window, spyglass in hand, watching koodoo down by the lake. "Ever shot a koodoos?" asked the wizard. The King had once been a master archer.

"Not much sport in hunting koodoos," replied the King, "danger doesn't excite me. Chasing Butterflies. Now that's a sport." The two men talked sports into the afternoon of the following day, as the King licked his all-day sucker.

14

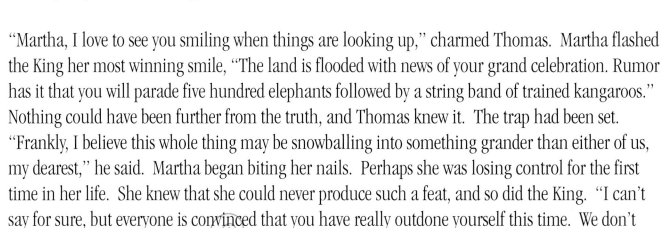

The year 2000 was going to arrive whether or not Thomas did anything on his own to acknowledge it. The party plans were going well. Perhaps, too well. The King and his cronies wished to insure that the focus on Chasing Butterflies would not be lost. "What is life without Chasing Butterflies?" wondered Thomas. Perhaps the Queen had shifted too much attention from the central event by planning so many other happenings. "We must think of a means to allow the Queen to have our way," Thomas said. The wizard was quick to support this line of thinking. If the party were to be a success, Chasing Butterflies would need to be at the heart of it. Together, we had to convince the Queen. The brothers discussed our options and a plan was hatched.

Thomas hummed a silly tune as he searched the palace looking for his Queen:

The court on a wing is a curious thing.
Only the King can make them sing.
I would give a pretty jeweled heart to see them fly.
If they can take wing, then so can I.

"Martha, I love to see you smiling when things are looking up," charmed Thomas. Martha flashed the King her most winning smile, "The land is flooded with news of your grand celebration. Rumor has it that you will parade five hundred elephants followed by a string band of trained kangaroos." Nothing could have been further from the truth, and Thomas knew it. The trap had been set. "Frankly, I believe this whole thing may be snowballing into something grander than either of us, my dearest," he said. Martha began biting her nails. Perhaps she was losing control for the first time in her life. She knew that she could never produce such a feat, and so did the King. "I can't say for sure, but everyone is convinced that you have really outdone yourself this time. We don't wish to disappoint, now do we?"

Martha's nostrils flared, and she grabbed at her chest looking like she might collapse from an attack of nerves at any moment. The King baited her by suggesting, "We might shift the focus from the country's outrageous expectations for your party by simply making a Kingly declaration." Martha could generally read Thomas like a book, but there were moments when he was a masterful actor. What the King was about to announce was the wizard's idea, but he dare not tell that to Martha. The King's eyes glistened as he rubbed his hands together in the delight of a truly good scheme about to unfold.

15

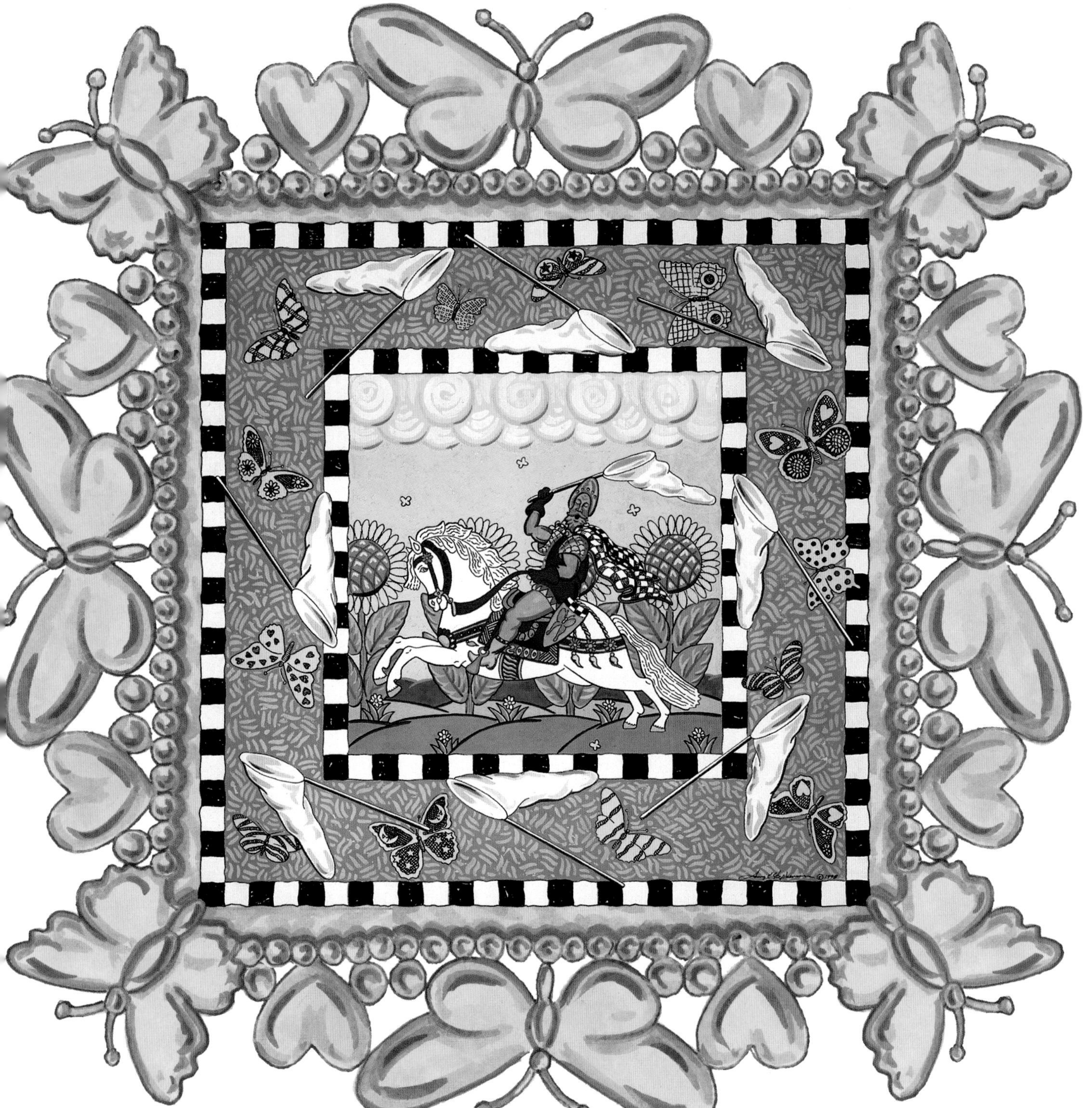

"We need to create additional excitement among the commonwealth," explained the King. "Stir things up a bit and divert attention, if only for a moment."

"How would you suggest we do this, my love?" questioned his Queen. The spider had woven his web and was about to close in on his prey.

"By offering a contest prize so grand that five hundred elephants could never compare."

The Queen had regained her composure and was now casually filing down her chewed nails. "Tell me more, Thomas," prompted the Queen, "you have wonderful insights into such matters." She was laying a trap of her own. I could see that she now realized Wizz was involved. From her point of view, the wizard's involvement meant the King would be incapable of upstaging anything she was planning.

"Momentary diversion is key," stated the King. The King could be correct about that part of his plan. Each continued to dabble in their superficial game of cat and mouse. Once more, Martha lent Thomas her ear. "I will offer a Royal Jeweled Heart to any man, woman, or child in the kingdom of Mill capable of capturing a Checkered Beauty and delivering it in time for the Millennium party." There, he had said it. This meant giving away a portion of his personal wealth, something Thomas had never done.

"And are you genuinely willing to produce such a wonderful prize?" the Queen asked. A Royal Heart embellished with rare gems would mean immediate wealth and status to the recipient. Gems were uncommonly scarce since all the Widgins who mined them had long since disappeared.

"Kooky-doo, what's a King to do?" Thomas sputtered total nonsense.

"But will you honor your promise, just in case this cherished creature is found?" the Queen interrogated.

"Wizz says that it cannot matter," the King retorted, "Checkered Beauties are the rarest butterflies known to Millennians. No one alive has really ever seen one. This is the kind of thing of which myths and fairy tales are made." Checkered Beauties adorned many a knight's armament. The black and white checks of the court derived their origin from these scarcest of all butterflies. Whether fact or fiction, many believed them to still exist.

Thomas Max seldom dealt well with reality, and he was not about to start now. I am sure he never planned to actually give away one of his uncommon hearts. I knew that if by a quirk of fate anyone did produce a Checkered Beauty, Thomas would reinterpret his declaration. He would find a way to add the Beauty to his collection on the palace walls and make up an excuse why he could not give away the heart. But he didn't disclose this nasty secret to his spouse. His trophy butterfly collection would be completed by such an acquisition, and that thought made Thomas very happy. It was not unusual in those days for people to want things they could not

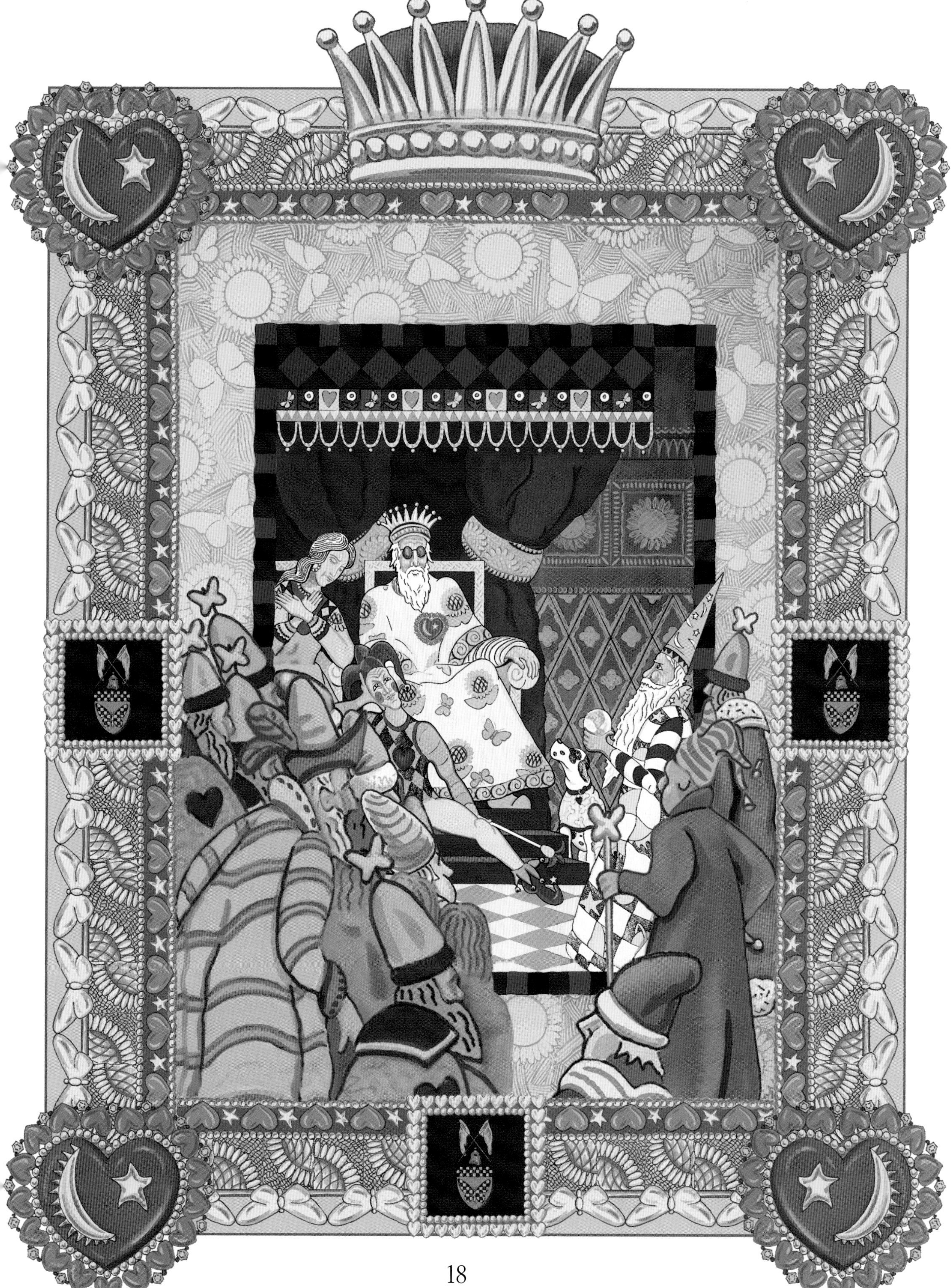

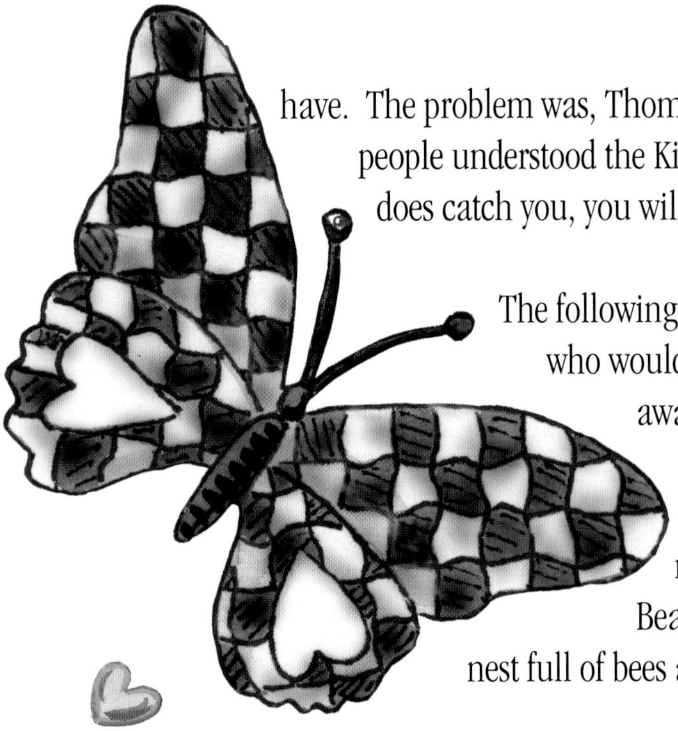

have. The problem was, Thomas was willing to do almost anything to get his way. Few people understood the King's deepest thoughts, "Butterfly, my oh my, if someone does catch you, you will die."

The following day the King's criers set out across the land telling anyone who would lend an ear, "Hear ye! Hear ye! A Royal Heart will be awarded to anyone who can present the King a Checkered Beauty in honor of the Millennium!" Before a dog could wag its tail, the entire countryside was covered with netsmen on horseback looking for the elusive Checkered Beauty. All came up empty. Still, the kingdom looked like a nest full of bees as people scoured the countryside in quest of their prize.

The King watched from his tower window where he and our brotherhood of friends drank our tea. "Nothing to do but wait," said the King. We all watched as the entire kingdom continued to waste one day into the next Chasing Butterflies. The kingdom was on verge of total collapse. No one was tending the farms. Not a cow was milked or a seed planted. Days stretched into weeks as Thomas enjoyed the sport from his tower window. All appeared normal through his tinted glasses.

A month went by before Rhubarb climbed the tower steps to inquire of the wizard, "Do Checkered Beauties even exist?" Rhubarb, the book reader, wanted facts.

"Not a one has been seen for a thousand years. Few before then, and none since," the wizard answered bluntly.

This told Rhubarb very little. "I wish a book on legends and myths," replied Rhubarb. Wizz pointed a crooked finger in the direction of a set of hand-carved-leather books that had obviously not been opened for decades. They were buried under centuries of dust, and the titles were no longer legible without furious scrubbing. "Where would I find a history of the legendary Checkered Beauty?" inquired Rhubarb. Wizz was the oldest resident of the castle. If anyone remembered, he would.

"The Book of Knowledge," stated Wizz. "But that is a book you will not find here."

"Then where will I find such a fable?"

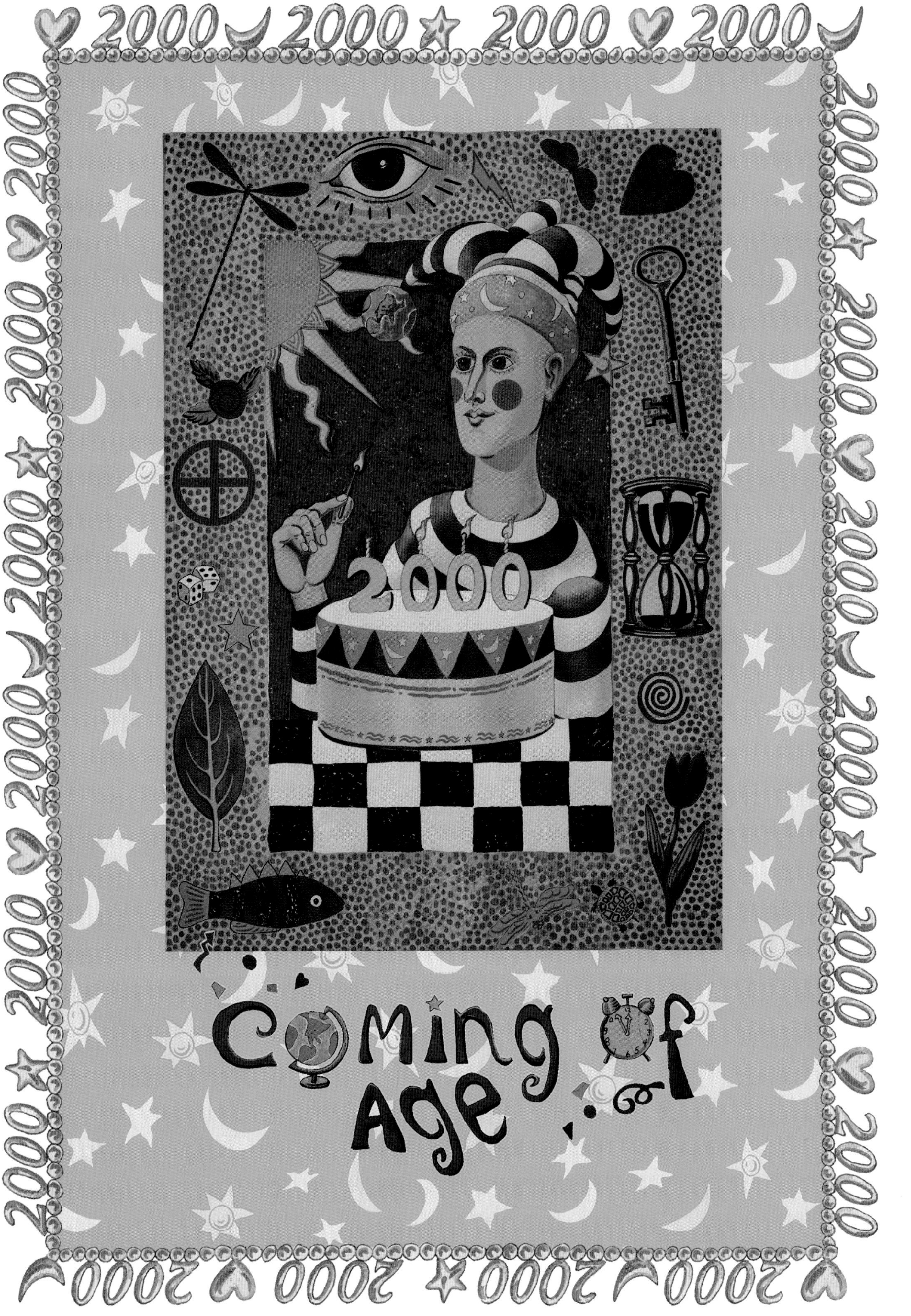
2000 2000 2000 2000
2000
Coming of Age

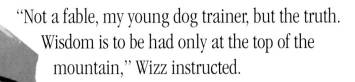

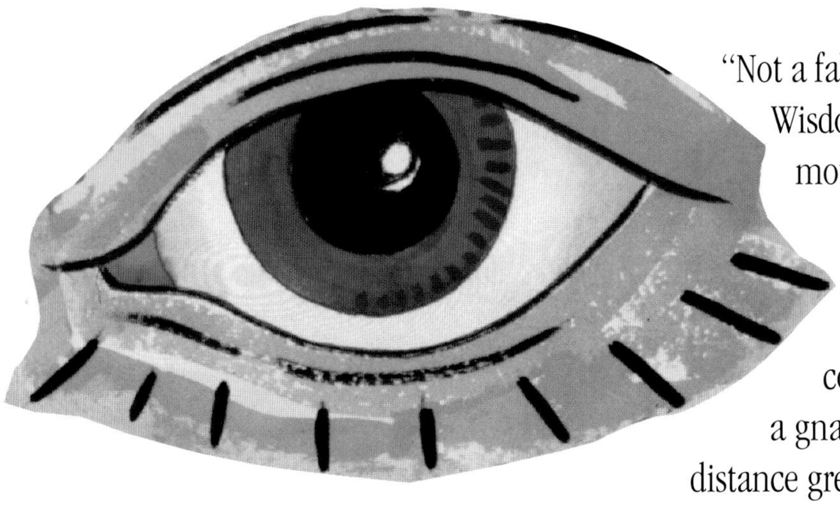

"Not a fable, my young dog trainer, but the truth. Wisdom is to be had only at the top of the mountain," Wizz instructed.

Surely, I thought, no wisdom still existed in the land of Mill. But where could truth be found? The wizard pointed a gnarly finger out the tower archway. In the distance grew a mountain from the foot of the village. "You must first climb to the top of Mt. Oculus," the old magician said before reaching down and dusting off *The Legend of Fables and Myths*. An eye was stamped in gold on its cover. "Take this to study. It will guide your way," he uttered as he blew off a whirlwind of dust and handed the book to Rhubarb. Rhubarb could have sworn that the eye on the cover winked at him as he took possession of the book.

*T*hus begins the rest of our story. Much of what
is recorded to Legend appears exactly as Rhubarb
told his own tale.

The Eye winked.

The book was born of the spirit. Rhubarb read as if under a spell. His fingers caressed every page as he read. A Watchful Eye has always looked down on the kingdom of Mill. He has taken many forms, both physical and ethereal.

Rhubarb knew that, historically speaking, an eye had always portrayed the all-knowing God. The people of Mill were generally uncertain as to their own religion. Gods were selected by convenience rather than by conviction. And through the years, all truth had become lost and replaced by frivolous games. Fables and myths usually shrouded the gods in mystery. This, however, had a different ring to it.

21

Rhubarb read on, "The Eye is always around you. He is always above you. He is there beside you when you need him. The Eye is the love in every beating heart." What was a beating heart? Rhubarb told me that as he read on, new words began to appear on the pages. The effect was spellbinding. The book had a life of its own, and the pages started to turn by themselves as the written word began to speak to him, "There, where the mountain meets the sky, you will find true wisdom. A Watchful Person will guide your way. A Wise Man holds the key at the top of the great mountain." Rhubarb listened intently. "Be true to yourself. Once you understand what truth is, then you can understand your own life. This is an ever-expanding loop." Jolts of electricity shot up Rhubarb's arm and charged his brain. Did this mean that he could find truth? In doing so, could he transfer such wisdom to his King?

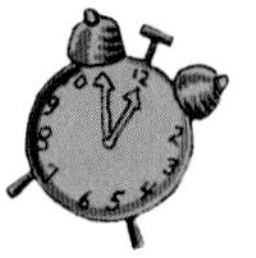

Held captive by distant mountain ranges on three of its borders, the land of Mill was married to the sea on another. Nestled safely into this hidden valley, the Millennians had remained isolated from the outside world since time began. Only the Widgins had ventured to cross through the rugged mountain passes with their trading caravans. Snow-capped mountains were chiseled from a block of endless granite north of the kingdom. South, a vast carpet of flowers stepped up onto the foothills of another mountain range not as jagged, but equally intimidating by the standards of all that lived in the valley. Never a ship had crossed the sea or explored its salty waters. To the east, the ground swelled and gave birth to a huge mountain snuggling up to the village - Mt. Oculus was without equal. As big from side-to-side as it was tall, Oculus linked the remaining distances between the other two mountain ranges. Foothills cascaded across the valley floor.

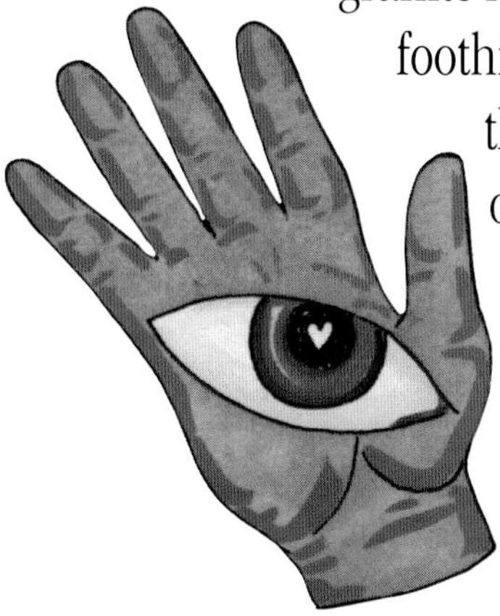

Could the Eye live at the top of Mt. Oculus? From there Rhubarb would be able to see the world. "Find your own truth," a voice whispered in the young dog trainer's ear, "go, climb the mountain." The book vibrated in Rhubarb's hand.

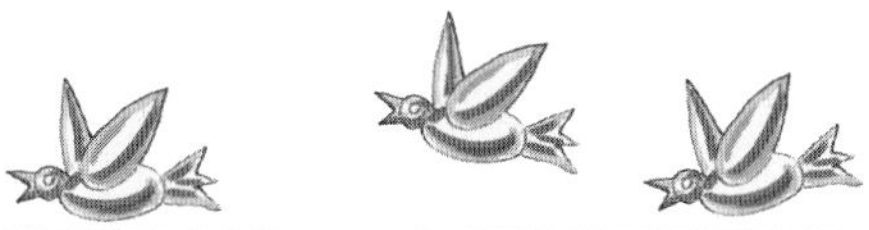

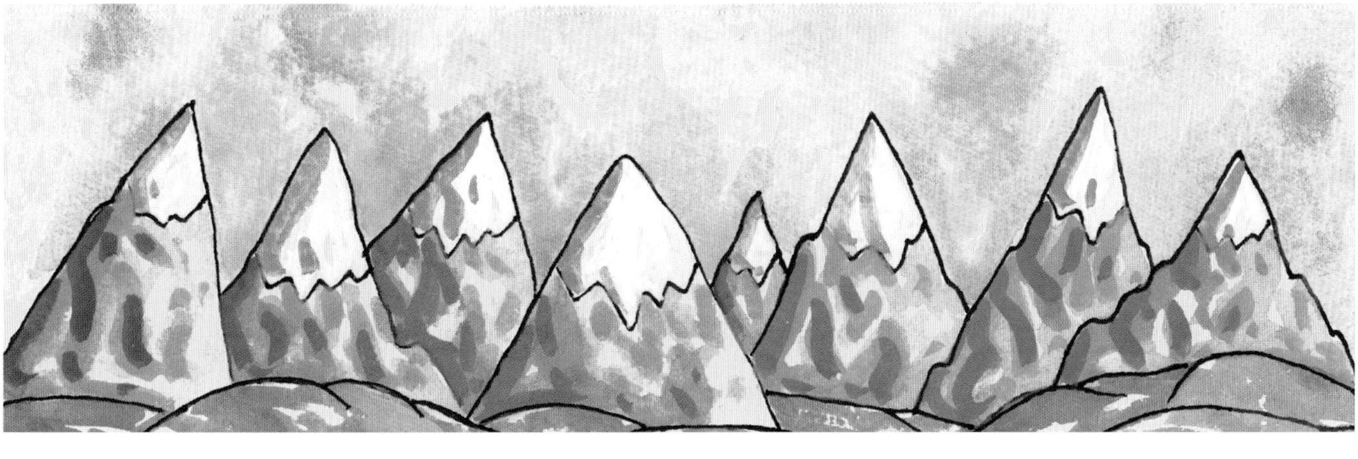

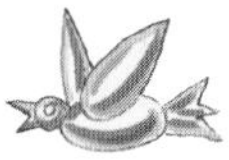

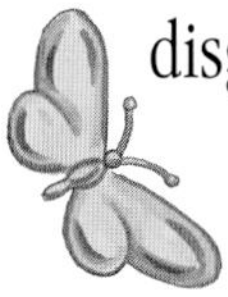

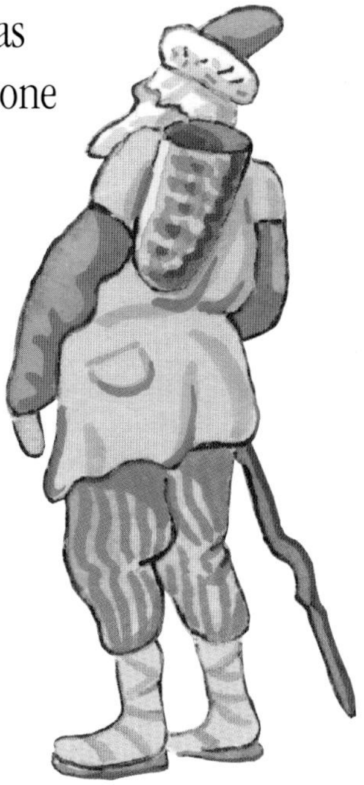

The next day Rhubarb met the Watchful Person on the village streets. He was disguised as a very old man shabbily dressed. He hobbled along the cobblestone streets bent by the heavy load of supplies he was carrying on his back. Rhubarb stopped and asked the man if he needed help with his burden. The street was swamped with people scurrying through the crowd in the Market Square. The load was stacked high on the elderly man's back, and Rhubarb thought the man might stumble at any moment. The man's eyes were the color of sapphires. He stared through Rhubarb as if he were gazing through water. An eerie feeling came over Rhubarb. "Thank you for asking," replied the Watchful Person, "I have been making this same journey for many years. You are the first kind soul to offer assistance. Perhaps you would like to walk with me to the edge of the village where the mountain begins its ascent. I live at the top of the mountain." The man winked and was on his way.

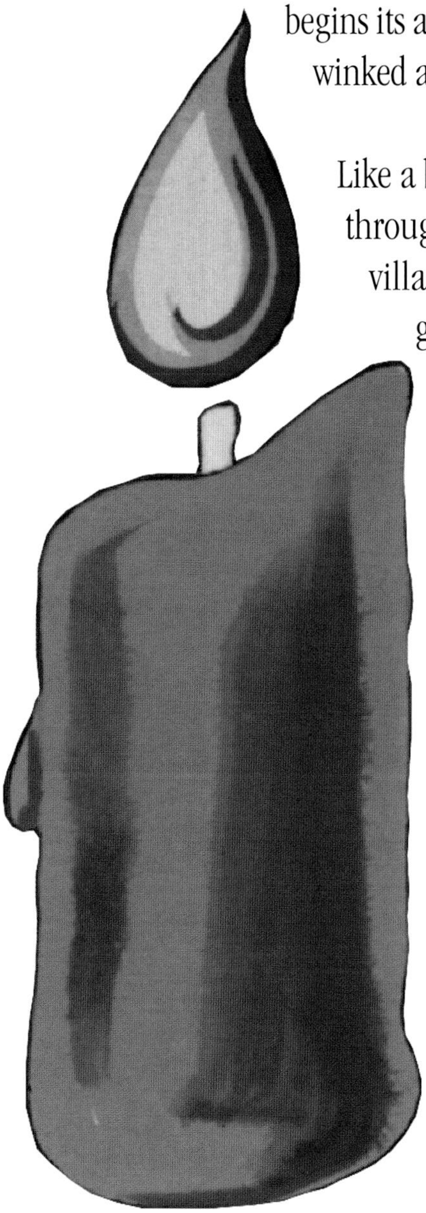

Like a burning candle, Rhubarb melted in behind the old man and followed him through the crowded streets. Together, they talked and walked to the edge of the village where the lane became a path before it was finally absorbed into a sea of green grass and daisies lapping at their knees. With the village at their backs, the two of them waded out into the field, which spilled onto the mountain steps.

Rhubarb could see cliffs and a much more formidable climb ahead. The path became steep and Rhubarb struggled to keep up. "Do you have fear of cats and koodoos?" panted Rhubarb. Cats were known to roam the mountain cliffs. Koodoos could be almost anywhere. Sweat poured from his brow and air was getting scarce. "Do wild boars ever block your path?" Rhubarb's questions were many. Should a boar wish to share their narrow trail, the drop could be fatal.

The Watchful Person looked back over his shoulder before answering, "Be true to your own spirit and soul. Animals know your soul." Rhubarb was like a child that asked too many questions. The old man sauntered up the mountain ahead of Rhubarb as his pace quickened.

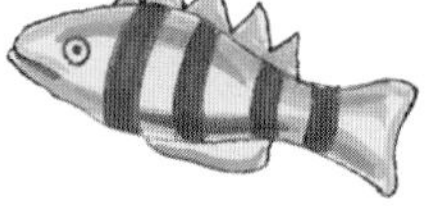

Rhubarb told me a most frightening story. What little air remained was suddenly choked off by a smell so foul it burned deep into Rhubarb's nostrils. A koodoo had vaulted from a nearby rock onto the tiny path they all three shared. The hairy creature was covered by large, black spots on a field of white. It landed on its hind legs with its arms and hooves extended in the air. Beady little eyes starred back at them. Grotesque lips parted into a smile that made Rhubarb gasp a second time. The stench of rotting flesh clung to its teeth. No more than an arm's length away, and no room for retreat, Rhubarb knew that death was near.

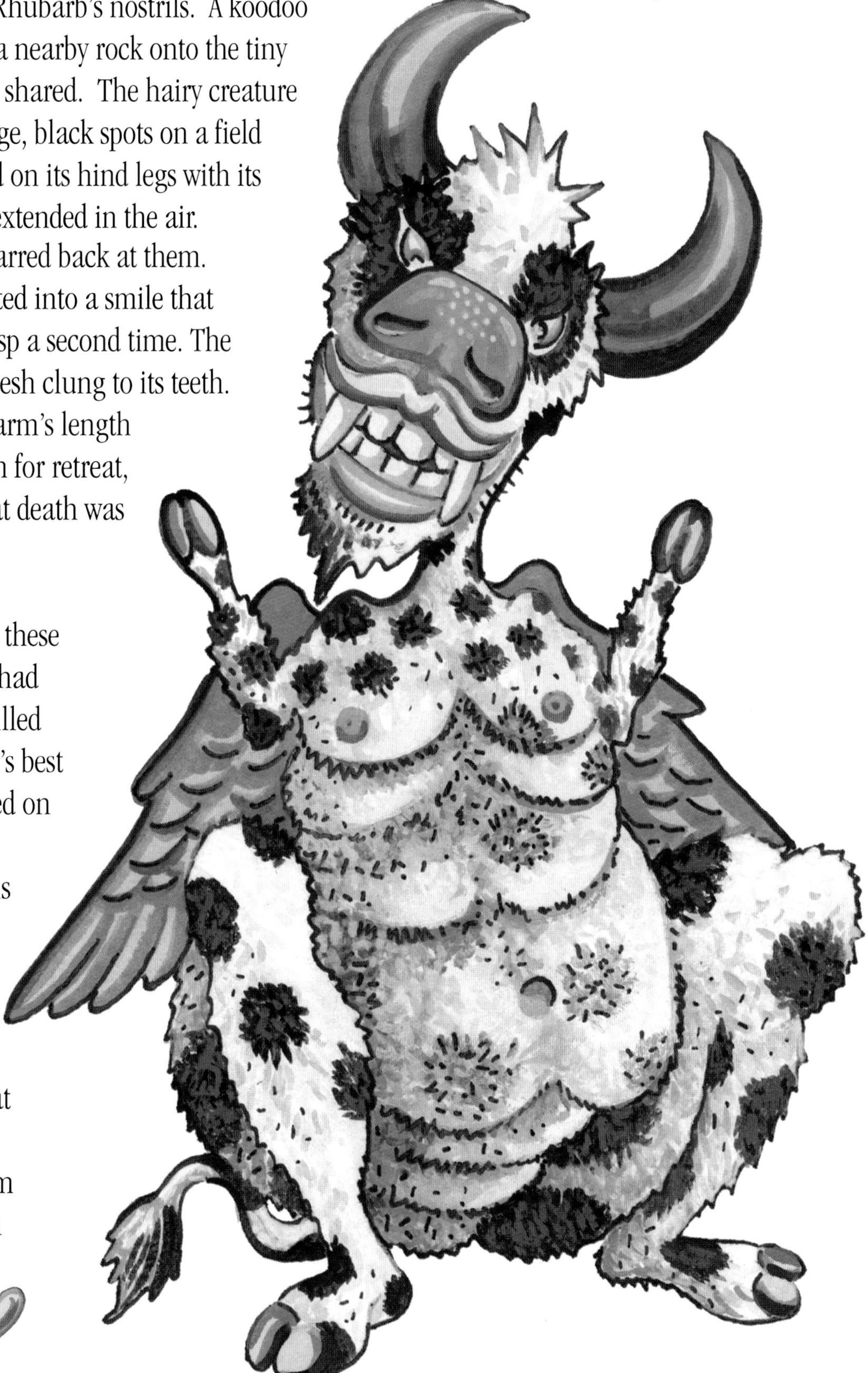

Legend had it that these hideous monsters had single-handedly killed armies of the King's best men when cornered on a path no larger than this one. This was a bull koodoo with wings - the worst possible kind! He could have taken flight at any moment and knocked them from their narrow perch into the abyss below.

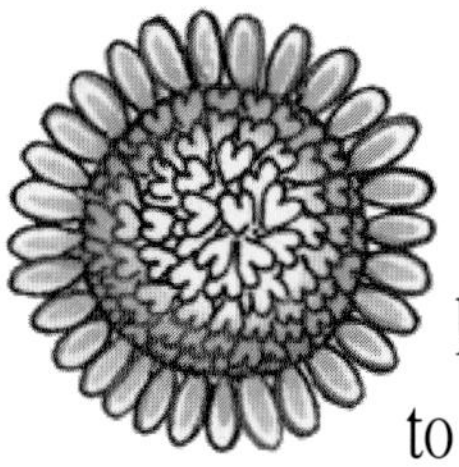

The old man held out but a finger and looked deep into the animal's eyes. The koodoo crouched before him and bowed its ugly head. The two climbers were allowed to pass. Rhubarb breathed a sigh of relief as he continued up the mountain with the koodoo far below them. How could it be that they were both spared to live another day? The two had just stared death in the face.

As they climbed skyward, everything appeared to be more luminous. The pair was nearing the crest of the mountain where the sky was painted yellow. "From where does the bright light reflect?" asked Rhubarb.

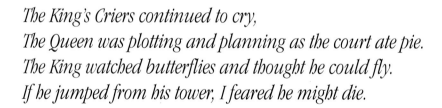

"It arises from the Land of Knowledge," answered the old man. An intense glow radiated beyond the mountain's crest into the heavens above. This light appeared to be bubbling up from the other side. In the distance, a hint of smoke whispered above the treetops. It brushed against the sky before disappearing as it faded into thin air. At that moment the path widened and opened into a small clearing where hand-chiseled steps appeared in the underlying granite. A well-manicured path lined by red tulips wound to the front door of a small cottage nestled against a rocky slope. The two walked to the front door and paused before stepping inside.

I am reminded as I commit this story to *The Legend of Fables and Myths,* that while Rhubarb was focused on scaling the mountain, the kingdom was growing more chaotic:

The King's Criers continued to cry,
The Queen was plotting and planning as the court ate pie.
The King watched butterflies and thought he could fly.
If he jumped from his tower, I feared he might die.

Those still sane among us hoped Rhubarb would return home soon with the answer of truth. The Clock was clicking into the Millennium.

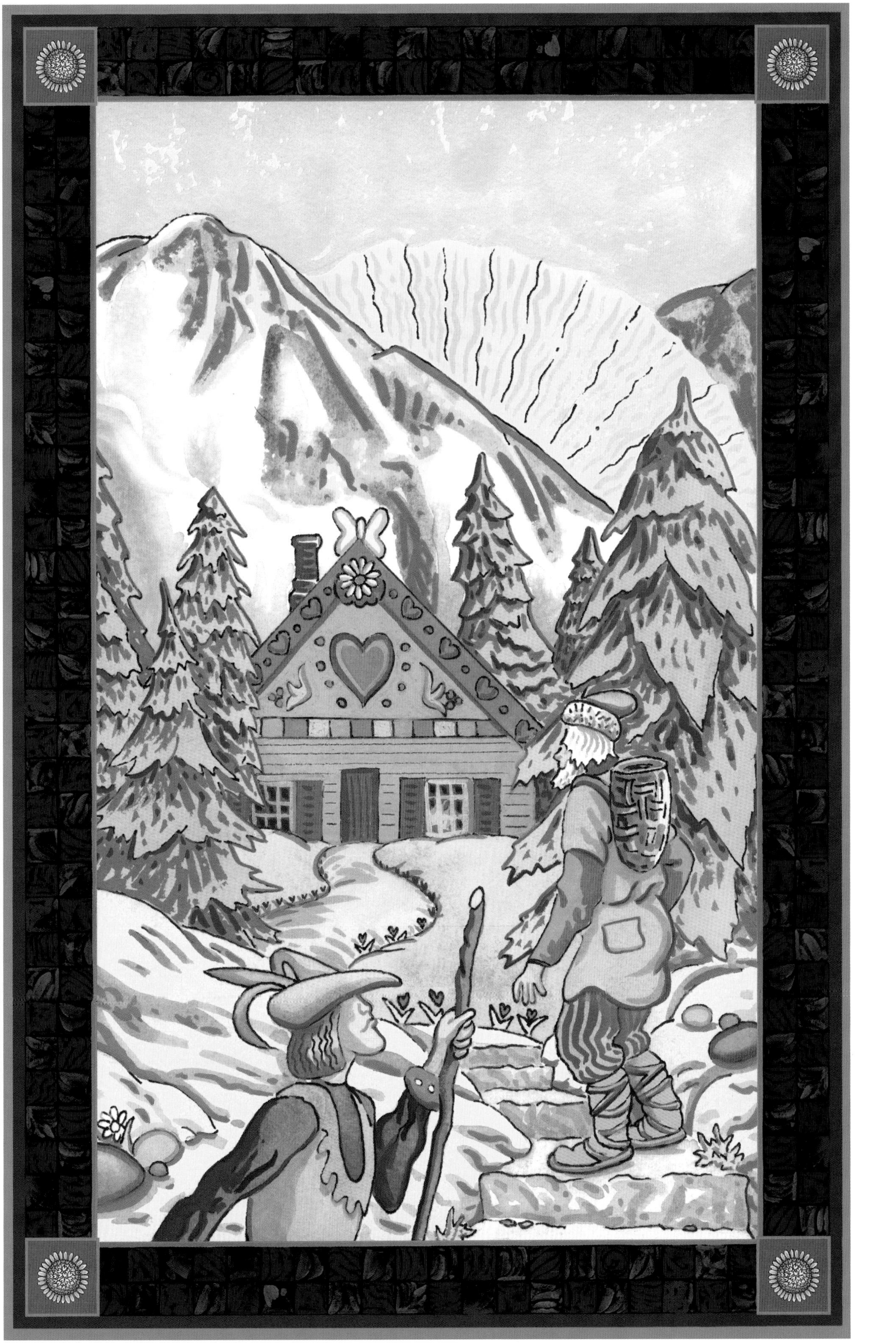

As the two travelers entered the small cottage, Rhubarb was filled with a warmth he had never experienced before. What had appeared to be a rather humble dwelling on the exterior was actually palatial inside. The entry hall had a vaulted ceiling with a gold chandelier hanging from a twenty-foot chain. A winding staircase cantilevered out from stone walls above the marbled floors and circled up several stories. "How could this be?" asked Rhubarb. The old man gave no answer. What had appeared to be a small cottage was mammoth in size.

After inviting Rhubarb into the formal library, the old man motioned to an over-stuffed wing chair studded with brass nails in the shape of eyes and welted with leather trim. He offered Rhubarb a place to sit and excused himself momentarily. As Rhubarb sank back into plush, down cushions, he began to absorb the details of his new surroundings. To Rhubarb's liking, the room was filled with books from floor to ceiling. Many were bound with similar carved-leather covers like the book Rhubarb carried inside his shirt. Each wall not plastered with books was decorated with painted portraits. Upon closer inspection, Rhubarb recognized some of the faces as people of the village. As Rhubarb looked on, the room began to grow. One room expanded into two, then three, and on and on. Portraits hung from every wall. "What can this be?" Rhubarb spoke to an empty room.

"Our growing family," answered a voice from above. Rhubarb saw nothing, as the room appeared empty of another soul. An eerie stillness crept into the room.

The silence was broken by soft footsteps across the oak floor. The person who now stood before Rhubarb was quite elegant and regal. He wore long flowing robes and was fitted with emerald slippers adorned with jewels like none Rhubarb had ever seen. No sewn-on hearts adorned this gentleman's clothing. Wisdom lined his face, and sophistication sparkled in his eyes.

Rhubarb tells that his mouth gaped. He felt as if he might suck in flies at any moment. Hanging from a velvet cord tied around the gentleman's neck was a large gold key. "You seek the Truth," said the scholar. Rhubarb couldn't speak as he stood awestruck. He could see the shine in this philosopher's eyes. "Much of it you have already. The rest you must earn. We all wish to be of one true spirit. Such mysteries of life seldom can be found in physical rewards. The Truth supplies the key." With that he vanished as quickly as he had come.

"The key! The key! Don't leave without giving me the key!" Rhubarb shouted back at an empty room full of books and paintings. The Wise Man had disappeared.

This was the Wise Man of myth and fable.

The old man reentered the room. "A meal before you retire, my young dog handler?" he inquired. Without time for an answer, the old man was on his way to the kitchen. Rhubarb hustled to keep up.

"The key of knowledge - of what good is it if I cannot have it?" asked a confused Rhubarb.

"You already have it. It is simply misplaced," his traveling partner answered emphatically. The old man proceeded into the kitchen where a small feast was prepared. "Eat well, young man, your journey lies ahead of you."

Rhubarb pounced on the food and gorged himself like a hungry animal. The hike up the mountain had burned an empty hole through the bottom of his stomach. Without further conversation, Rhubarb grabbed at the meal with both fists until he was completely satisfied. The hour of nod soon blanketed Rhubarb. Not needing to be led off to bed, Rhubarb succumbed on the kitchen table where he slept until morning.

I t was my duty as scribe to record the facts exactly as I observed them or as they were related to me firsthand. While Rhubarb was away, the King was at play.

Meanwhile, back at the palace, a parade was about to take place at the stroke of midnight. The entire court was lined up in their pajamas about to do a bunny-hop up and down the tower stairs. This procession of idiots delighted the King.

Thomas was in his bathrobe thinking about you know who,
as Baby, dancing a jig, sang dippity-doo.
The queen was in committee feeling oh so blue,
if only there were an expert to tell her what to do.

The next day Rhubarb awoke to find the Wise Man sitting at the table eating his morning bowl of oats. Wisdom gleamed through the kitchen windows as light painted the room. Rhubarb came to attention as soon as he got his wits about him.

"A key?" asked Rhubarb. "*The Book of Knowledge*?" He posed both questions without waiting for an answer. Like a child he required too much too quickly.

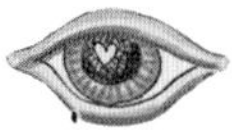

"You have all that you need. The book inside your shirt will guide the way," said the Wise Man speaking volumes within the two sentences. Again, he was gone.

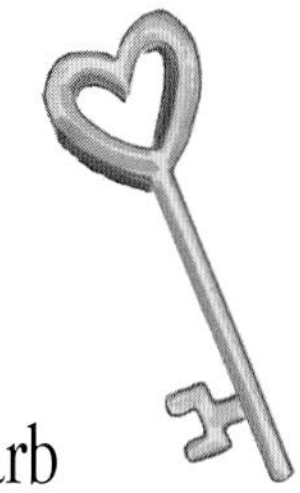

Rhubarb tells a magical tale. He felt something urging him to pull the leather book from inside of his shirt. The eye on its outside cover had just come to life. The book watched Rhubarb intently as Rhubarb turned a page and another illustration came to life. Rhubarb could see a beautiful valley awash in a sea of bright yellow sunflowers standing shoulder to shoulder. Rhubarb rubbed at his eyes and imagined that he could smell the flowers growing right out of the pages of the book. Some were a bit twisted; others stooped or bent over just like the old man. Occasionally, one was beautiful and perfect, but not too often. Each flower seemed to be as individual as every person he knew. Checkered butterflies flew from flower to flower.

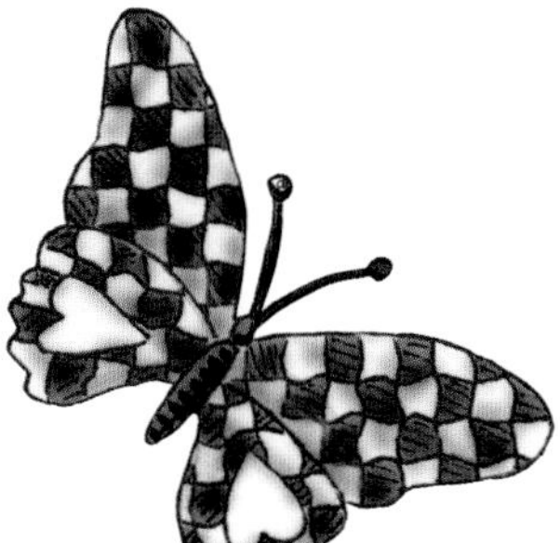

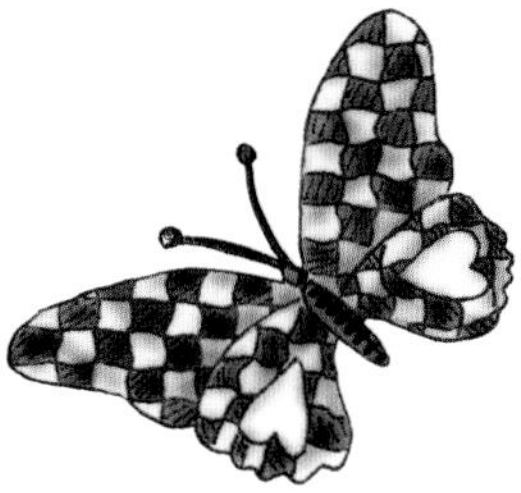

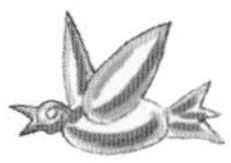

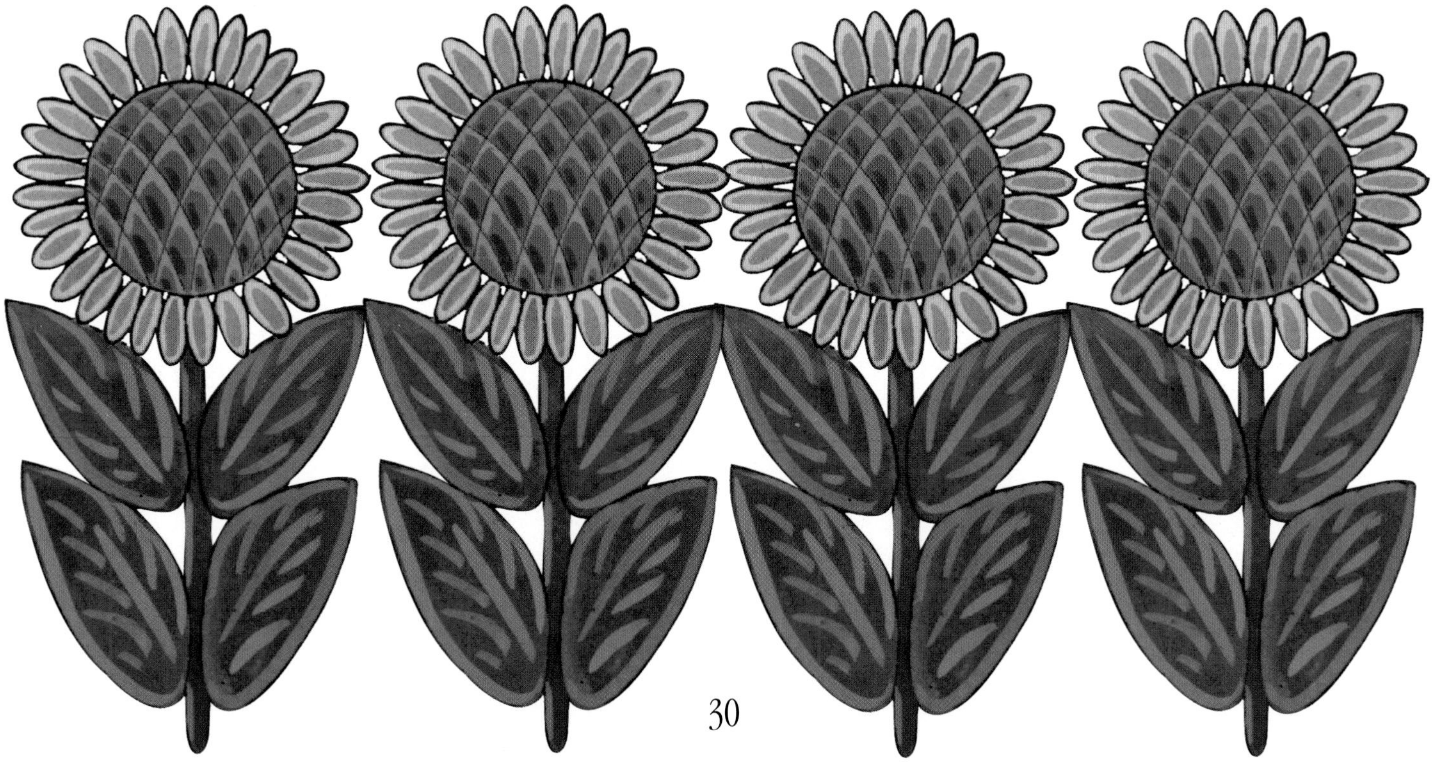

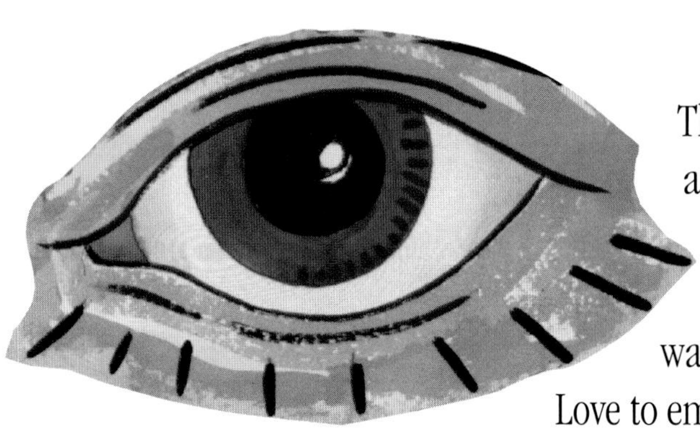

Then the book began to speak, "Let me introduce myself. I am the all-powerful Eye. Maker of the Heavens. God of the Galaxies. In the beginning The Eye created all that was good. He created Truth to run pure like crystal waters. Knowledge to spring forth for those who seek it. Love to embrace those who preach it. The source of all these things is in the heart. Without them, the heart is empty."

"Is this what you mean by a heart?" asked Rhubarb gesturing to the piece of fabric sewn to his chest. He thought it could not be of so much importance.

"Your heart beats life when you connect with your own soul," stated the Eye.

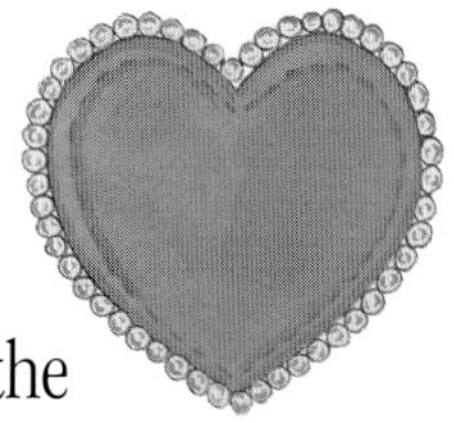

The book paused and turned a page. Another picture appeared to be showing the future. Rhubarb could see his own face peering over large yellow flowers inside the book. Checkered Beauties were at play. The book went on, "All creatures have value. Even a gnat that specks the sky, a whale that swims the sea, a bird that learns to fly, or a man who dares to be. Everything serves its purpose. The moss beneath your feet. The stones upon the ground. The oats you get to eat. The melodies of sound. All things serve their purpose. Each is a gift of the Eye."

The book continued, "Rhubarb, your quest remains before you. It is yours to discover. Find truth and you will learn the answers you seek."

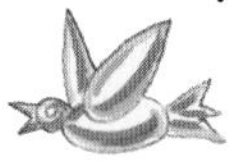

"Cross to the other side of the mountain," appeared in bold print at the bottom of the page. Then the book closed upon itself. The Eye winked, and the book became lifeless.

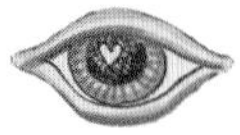

The old man appeared at the door. "I will guide you through the snows to the mountain crest. The paths are heavy with snow and may be laced with ice. Fall from the path, and you may be lost forever," the old man ominously cautioned.

Together, they started up where they had left off the day before. The climb proved slow, but the mountaineers made good time. At mid-day, Rhubarb looked down from the crest of Oculus into the Land of Knowledge.

"Remember, my young dog handler, that we are all connected in a much greater circle. You are

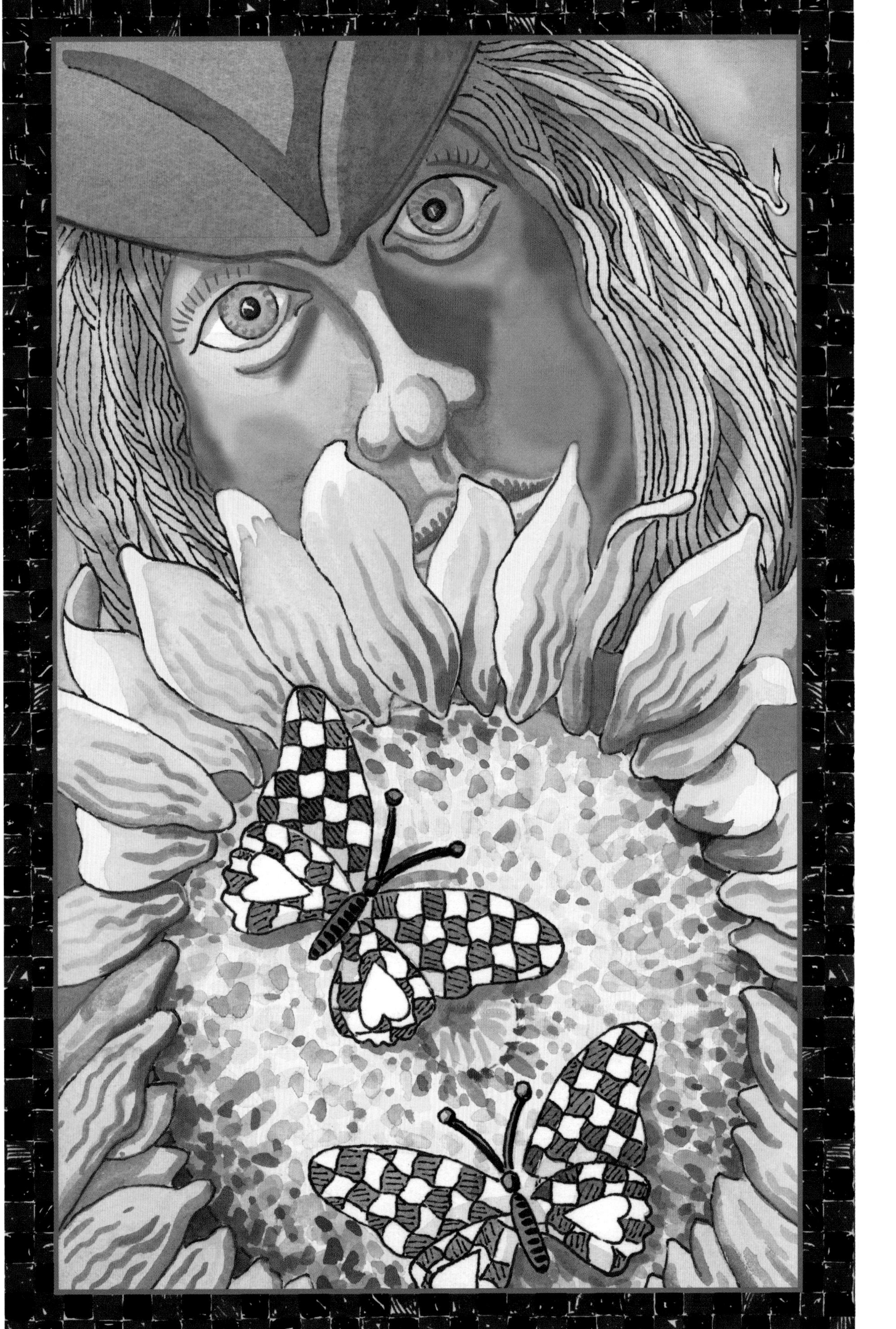

but a link in the chain. The chain's strength comes from every link. Each link has its worth, but no link alone can hold the chain together. Search and you will find your place in the chain. That is your Truth," the old man advised. Then they started down the mountain.

"Is that all?" yelled Rhubarb.

"We each seek our own truth," replied the old man. "Go find yours. I cannot lead you to it." He rounded a bend in the mountain and disappeared, not to be seen again.

So it had come to pass. Rhubarb had met a Watchful Person who tamed a killer koodoo, found the fabled Wise Man, and conversed with a book - all in a night and a day. He had climbed the feared Mt. Oculus to its crest and looked down into the Land of Knowledge on its other side. No Millennian had imagined such feats! Far below Rhubarb on the other side, the people of Mill chased butterflies, genuine and surreal.

"What of this is real? What is dream? Who knows the Truth?" Rhubarb questioned himself as he descended into the sea of yellow. "Is there a greater meaning to life than Chasing Butterflies?" Emeralds and rubies sparkled beneath his feet. Bright light was everywhere. His path was steep as he began to approach the valley floor. All at once Rhubarb's feet slipped out from under his lanky body, and he rolled like a tumbleweed down the remaining hillside into a patch of gargantuan sunflowers. Huge, mansized sunflowers grew everywhere like the ones painted in the illustration of his book. They threw off an immense yellow light. Rhubarb had never seen anything like it. There, where the land met the sky, fluttered two Checkered Beauties, like shining specks of hope hanging over the horizon.

They floated down on outstretched wings landing on the flower in front of Rhubarb's nose. "Whoosh!" Was it the sound of Rhubarb sucking in air as he held his breath in anticipation or were the butterflies so close he could actually hear them pass? Their wings unfolded like multiple chessboards. "The checkers of the court," exclaimed Rhubarb under his breath as a light went off in his brain! A heart was etched into the checkerboard on the butterfly's lower wing. Instinct told Rhubarb to reach out and grab one, but he did not. It was as if he were in a hypnotic state.

"Do you love me?" echoed from somewhere in the stratosphere.

Rhubarb felt for the book inside his shirt. Perhaps, the book was talking to him. "Do you love me?" the whisper repeated itself.

It is my duty as scribe to record history as accurately as possible. Although I was not actually present, I believe the following events did indeed happen exactly as Rhubarb has conferred them to me for inscription into this Legend of Fables and Myths. *This is how Rhubarb found his own meaning of truth.*

Then something totally trusting and unexpected happened. One of the Beauties flew over to Rhubarb and landed on his outstretched finger. The other fluttered about Rhubarb's head. These innocent insects had never been chased. They had no knowledge of the net or what it might represent. The thought of mounting one of these loving creatures to the King's wall totally sickened Rhubarb.

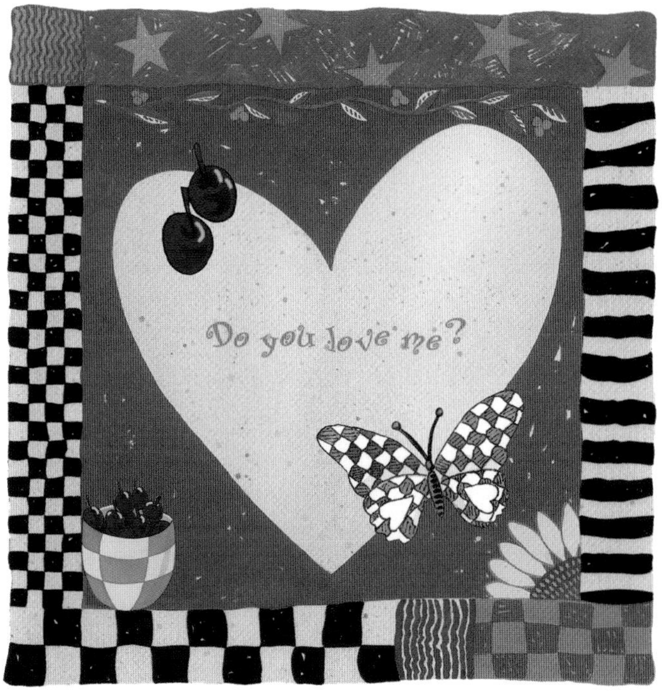
Do you love me?

Rhubarb leaned back and rested his head as the pair of Checkered Beauties fluttered around the toes of his boots. "What do I do?" asked Rhubarb. As he gazed out into the yellow sky, Rhubarb noticed that the expanse was polka-dotted with pairs of Beauties similar to the ones at his feet. "Why so many, yet none on the other side of the mountain?" Suddenly something occurred to him. "The checkerboard of the court, and the King's coat of arms - all were painted in black and white!" Rhubarb believed that these butterflies had influenced this ornamentation. "There must have been a great number of Checkered Beauties in Mill once upon two moons," explained Rhubarb. I agree with Rhubarb. What could have happened so long ago to cause the butterflies to disappear?

"Something must be done about this," shouted Rhubarb to the mountaintops! "Enough of Chasing Butterflies and wasting each day into the next!" If the Checkered Beauties had long since left the land of Mill, what else had escaped its boundaries?

"What is real? What is in dreams? Is life Chasing Butterflies all that it seems?" Rhubarb questioned the meaning of his own life:

What is of value? What is the cost?
What is worth keeping? What is lost?
What unlocks truth? Who holds the key?
Mill is the craziest kingdom there ever could be!

Rhubarb fell asleep. When he awoke, the butterflies were taking a nap on his shoulder. "You hold the key," a voice spoke from inside his shirt. The book had begun to feel quite warm and lifelike as the Eye nudged Rhubarb into conversation.

"Have I all along?" questioned Rhubarb.

"Everyone holds a key. The question is how they use it," spoke the Eye on the book.

"The question is, if they will use the key at all," answered Rhubarb. Rhubarb was talking to a book! It was becoming quite clear if the King were going to be etched into *The Legend of Fables and Myths* as anything greater than a bungling butterfly basher, he had best change his ways. Rhubarb loved his friend and King. More importantly, he wished him to take his rightful place in the records of time. The brotherhood shared this concern with Rhubarb. More importantly, the brotherhood shared something else much greater that had not come with an appointment. "True friendship grows out of love!" yelled Rhubarb. The brothers wanted their King to succeed.

This thought pacified Rhubarb the following day as he started back up the mountain with his two new friends circling about his shoulders. Together, they crossed over the mountain crest and negotiated the perilous ice fields without incident. On the way down the Mountain, Rhubarb and his butterfly companions came upon the koodoo. Rhubarb looked deep into the animal's eyes and touched its very being. The koodoo granted passage as Rhubarb and the two Checkered Beauties proceeded without fear. They camped within view of the village below and could see the campfires interspersed among a sea of tents extending from the castle walls.

The following morning Rhubarb crossed the field of daisies beyond the toe of the mountain and came upon an encampment of sword-swallowers waiting an audition with the Queen. Hot coals sent up wisps of smoke into the morning air. Warm days and nights had given way to an Indian summer. Fall

Then something truly wonderful occurred.

would soon envelop Mill. The gold of turning aspen trailed down the mountain. Men and women sat around campfires rubbing their hands and drinking hot broth poured from hammered copper kettles suspended over the coals. Children played at the edge of a bubbling brook that wound its way through this temporary city of tents and cots. Fire-eating clowns practiced their voluptuary feats with Epicurean delight as they wandered aimlessly among the crowd. A juggler as tall as a giraffe tossed bonbons into the air, catching and eating each one as he balanced on his stilts. Tattooed and bearded ladies, fortunetellers, animal trainers, fast-talkers, and loose women paraded among the crowd. Vendors sold everything the mind could imagine. Nothing had been left to chance.

Gourmet specialties were offered to tempt the most peculiar palates - snail pie, kitty gumbo, and pudding with eyes. Crow to eat, pickled mumbo jumbo, and koodoo meat. The Kookarotzi sold a long line of twisted trinkets as well as unnecessary sundries:

These eccentric vendors traded things like chicken teeth,
cat tails, canned bad breath and canary feet,
bagged eyelashes, powdered beaks,
long fingernails and braided leeks.
Painted baby ducks and butterfly wings,
these were a few of the most curious things.

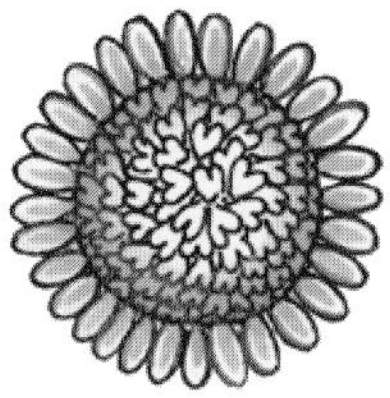

Rhubarb made his way through the encampment of peasantry and Kookarotzi - kooks as most knew them. He continued into the village where banners hung from every surface. The butterflies danced around his head and shoulders as he moved through the crowd of loonies, wackos, and screwballs, all in line to audition for the Queen. This collection of the unusual had proven quite entertaining for everyone in the village, and many had joined in the fun. No one paid Rhubarb any mind or noticed the Checkered Beauties floating around his head. Rhubarb was careful to keep the butterflies under his hat as he entered the city streets near the castle for fear they might end up on the palace walls.

As Rhubarb approached the royal residence, the King called down, "Open the gates!" A squadron of a thousand archers now lined the gates to keep out loonies at night and Kookarotzi during the day. Rhubarb was escorted over the bridge and into the Palace Square. A huge bandstand had been erected and a marble podium now stood next to the palace where the King and Queen gave speeches to selected guests.

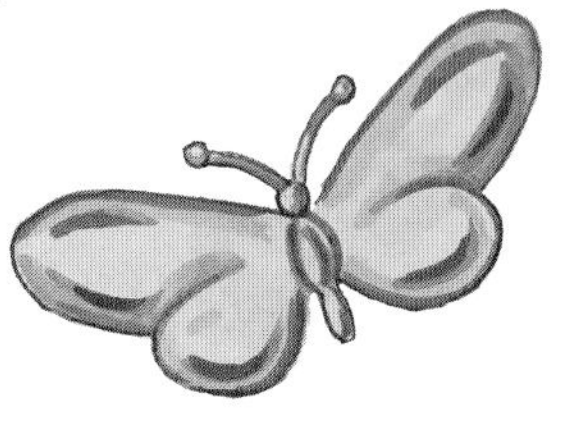

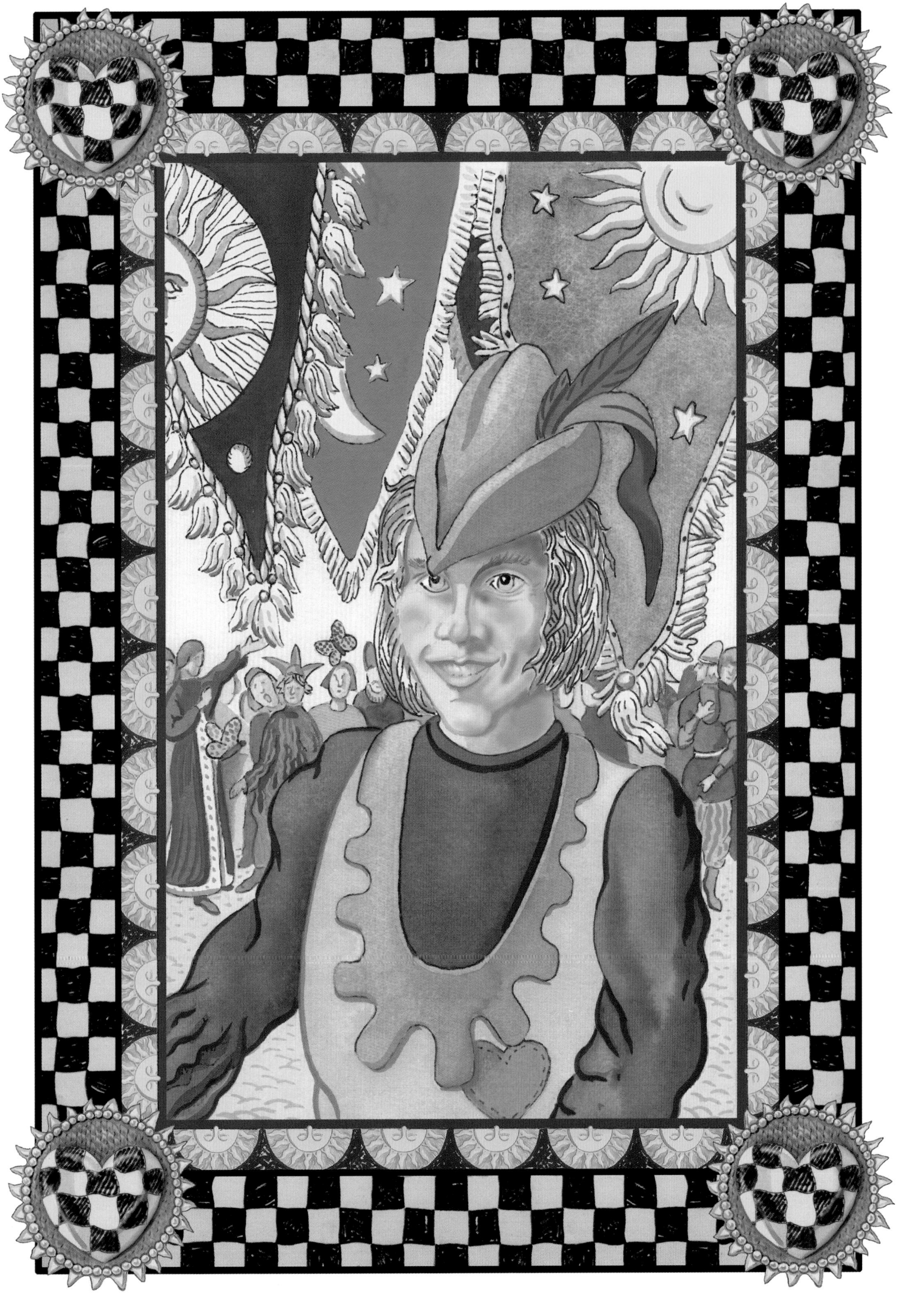

"A hero's welcome for my grand, young friend!" cried the King from across the square, "Soon we must eat, drink, and be merry, then talk of distant lands." The King knew nothing of what Rhubarb had under his hat, but expected something of value on Rhubarb's return. "Perhaps some idle conversation if nothing else," thought the King.

Baby ran towards Rhubarb dragging Wizz at the end of a leash. She hurtled into the air knocking Rhubarb to the ground and licking him until he was wet from head to heel. Rhubarb dusted himself off as he gave Baby a giant hug. Together they went to Rhubarb's room where he left his butterfly friends as he partied into the night.

A grand procession escorted Rhubarb to the throne room. The entire Court wished to hear his tales. As the King sat and listened, a feast was prepared in honor of Rhubarb's return.

A string band dressed in kangaroo costumes was playing delightful tunes, while a troop of trained dancers filed by in elephant suits parading trunk to tail.

"We call it the baby elephant walk," informed the Queen. The guest of honor stared in total amazement from his seat at the head table between his King and Queen.

"Try to recognize the members of the court…dressed like hopping bunnies with long ears and rabbit's noses! I think I just might cry," giggled the King beside himself.

Rhubarb could not believe the enormous effort that had gone into the senseless extravaganza. Rhubarb quietly pondered:

W hat is real?
What is dream?
Can life be as silly as it seems?

Just a practice party in your honor," glowed the Queen. "The Millennium will be ten-fold grander once all the auditions have been completed."

This hollow sickness had emptied the souls of almost everyone throughout the kingdom. "How many more auditions?" Rhubarb asked his Queen.

"Ten-thousand-and-four, not a gnats wing more," was the Queen's prompt response.

A thousand of the King's finest soldiers began parading through the tables with their hearts sewn upon their sleeves. This march joined baby elephants, kangaroos and hopping bunnies as it continued around the room to the music of the band. The homecoming quickly turned into pandemonium. Rhubarb was exhausted from his trip and asked to retire for the evening. "I am tired my King. My journey was long and my story will be even longer. I fear I must wait another day to share the details of my adventure."

The King stood and tapped his glass with a silver spoon he had just taken from his mouth, "A toast for our retiring hero." People clapped and cheered. "Tomorrow, Rhubarb tells his story on the King's podium in the Palace Square."

Rhubarb excused himself and returned to the privacy of his room. He put out a dish of sweet fruit drink he had taken from the party. The Checkered Beauties ate with mad delight while his head churned with worries, "How can I save these Beauties when they carry such a bounty on their heads?"

He tormented himself until late into the night when he drifted off into a fretful sleep. The next morning Rhubarb awoke to see the two exquisite beauties perched on his blanket. "How could anyone think of killing such trusting creatures?" mused Rhubarb. Suddenly, he began to feel an ache inside. It was at this moment he realized that no one with a real heart would be capable of extinguishing such loveliness to mount on a palace wall. Much more importantly, Rhubarb understood that the stirring at his breast was not coming from the heart sewn onto his shirt pocket. He had a real heart! How else could he feel the pounding inside his body? If Rhubarb had a heart, then he felt certain that others must have one too!

Bugles blared from the courtyard below. Rhubarb heard the King's Criers summoning the countryside to hear his tale. Time was growing short. Soon he must descend from his room and face the King with his truth:

Beauty cannot be manufactured, by King or peasant.
It cannot be captured, even if the vision is pleasant.
Beauty cannot be mounted on palace walls,
or strung across castle halls.
Beauty is having a purpose for everything you do.
It is concern for what happens to others more than what happens to you.
Beauty is giving and sharing
It is loving and caring.
Beauty is finding you are not alone.
It is finding the truth close to home…inside your soul.

I wish that I had been a statue in the corner when Rhubarb returned to his room. This record states to the best of my ability, those thoughts and feelings Rhubarb later related to me.

Rhubarb took off his hat and placed it on his dresser. He whistled softly and the two Checkered Beauties fluttered to his outstretched finger. Carefully raising the brim of the hat, he placed them underneath for safekeeping. Rhubarb believed that he must first tell his story before anyone learned of the pair's existence. If he couldn't convince his liege to give up the chase, then he would take them back where he had found them.

Slowly, Rhubarb headed down the stairs - carefully mulling over what he would say. As he emerged onto the Palace Square, his eyes grew large. Thousands of Millennians had pushed their way through the gates to hear from the traveler. In anticipation of a tale of mythic achievement, the crowd began to chant, "A heart for a hero, a heart for a boy!" Rhubarb nervously climbed the steps to the marble podium where the King, the Queen, Wizz and the kingdom of Mill waited for him. Rhubarb hoped he would adequately be able to express what he knew in his now-beating heart to be true. Life in Mill depended on it.

Just then, he heard the vibration of delicate wings. "Oh, the Beauties," he cried. They had escaped from his cap inside his room to join the party. Rhubarb raised his hand hoping to entice them to land in his protective care. But instead, they swooped up high above the crowd circling among the fluttering banners. Then they gracefully glided down and perched themselves in Rhubarb's hands. Rhubarb lifted them to the sky, but instead of fleeing for safety, they flew over and landed on the King's shoulders.

Rhubarb gasped. In total amazement, the King removed his rose-colored glasses. For the first time in years he could see clearly. Tears pooled in Thomas Max's eyes. The crowd clapped and roared. Yet, the butterflies remained calmly at his side. "What magnificence," he whispered. He cautiously lifted the Checkered Beauties and placed them on the marble podium above the crowd. Turning towards Rhubarb, Thomas Max put his arms around him and squeezed him tightly.

"These Checkered Beauties are a dream I have chased for many years," stammered the King. "I thought they would be the crowning acquisition for my collection. But to see them take flight. . .well, I can't imagine trying to contain that beauty. Thank you, my friend, for what you have brought."

Thomas Max looked up at Rhubarb, then reached down to remove the Jeweled Heart on his chest. Rhubarb quickly placed his hand over the King's, "Oh no, your majesty. I need nothing from you. I already have a heart. And now I know you do too." Rhubarb then stood before the crowd and tore the heart-shaped fabric from his chest!

The King felt a strange pounding inside his own chest. A low hum grew as people across the land started hearing their own hearts for the very first time. Everyone began tearing sewn-on hearts from their garments. The Wizz stepped forward and joined in the excitement almost ripping a hole in his robe.

The King shouted from the podium, "Let this day go down in history as the beginning of an age when every heart was filled with love!" Thomas Max could see now that every Millennian had a real heart all along. It simply took an act of love to fill it.

Fireworks thundered overhead. Dozens of court jesters, acrobats and jugglers mingled through the crowds. The King decreed that Rhubarb light the cake. Then the Queen linked arms with her King and his merry band of rogues as the Checkered Beauties circled above.

Thus ends my record. Herewith I commit to the sands of time my account of Thomas Maximus and his small band of friends who found what was of true value. Long live the Legends of Mill!

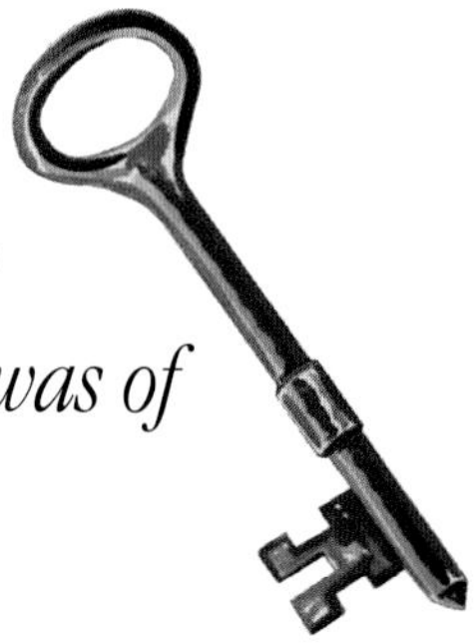

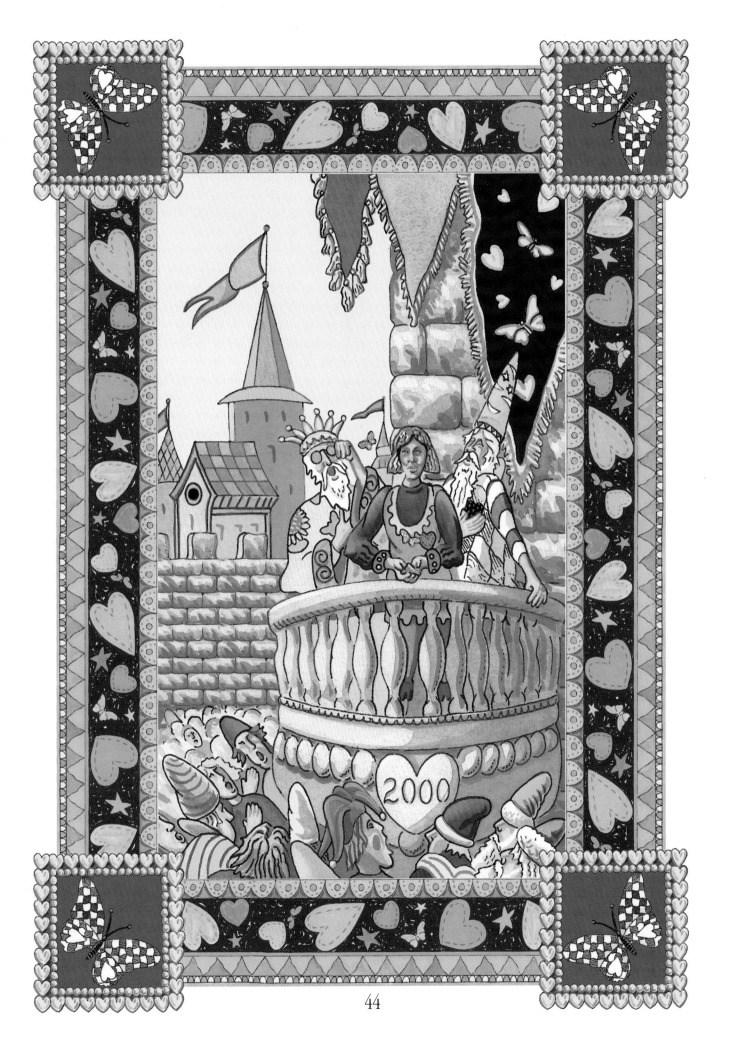

44

The End

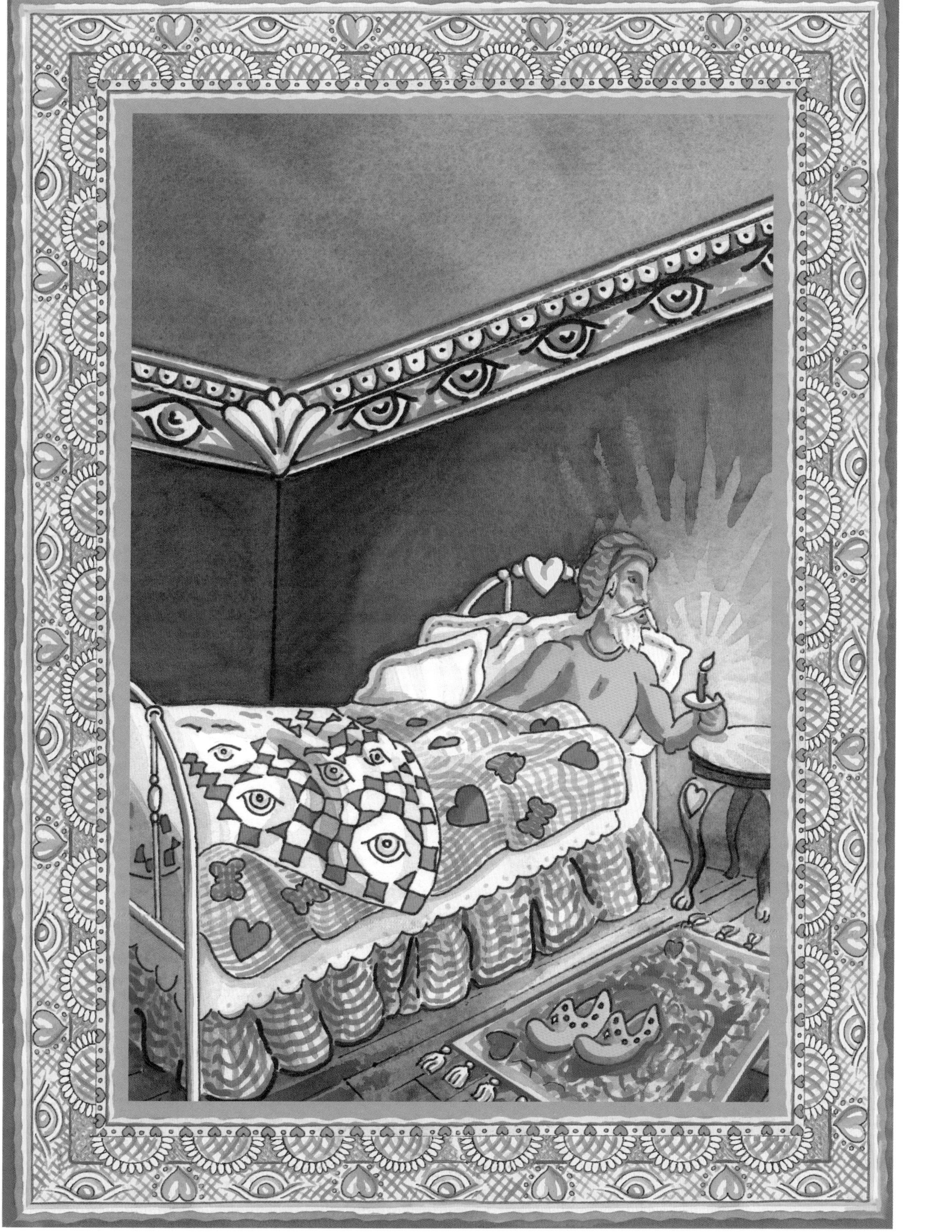

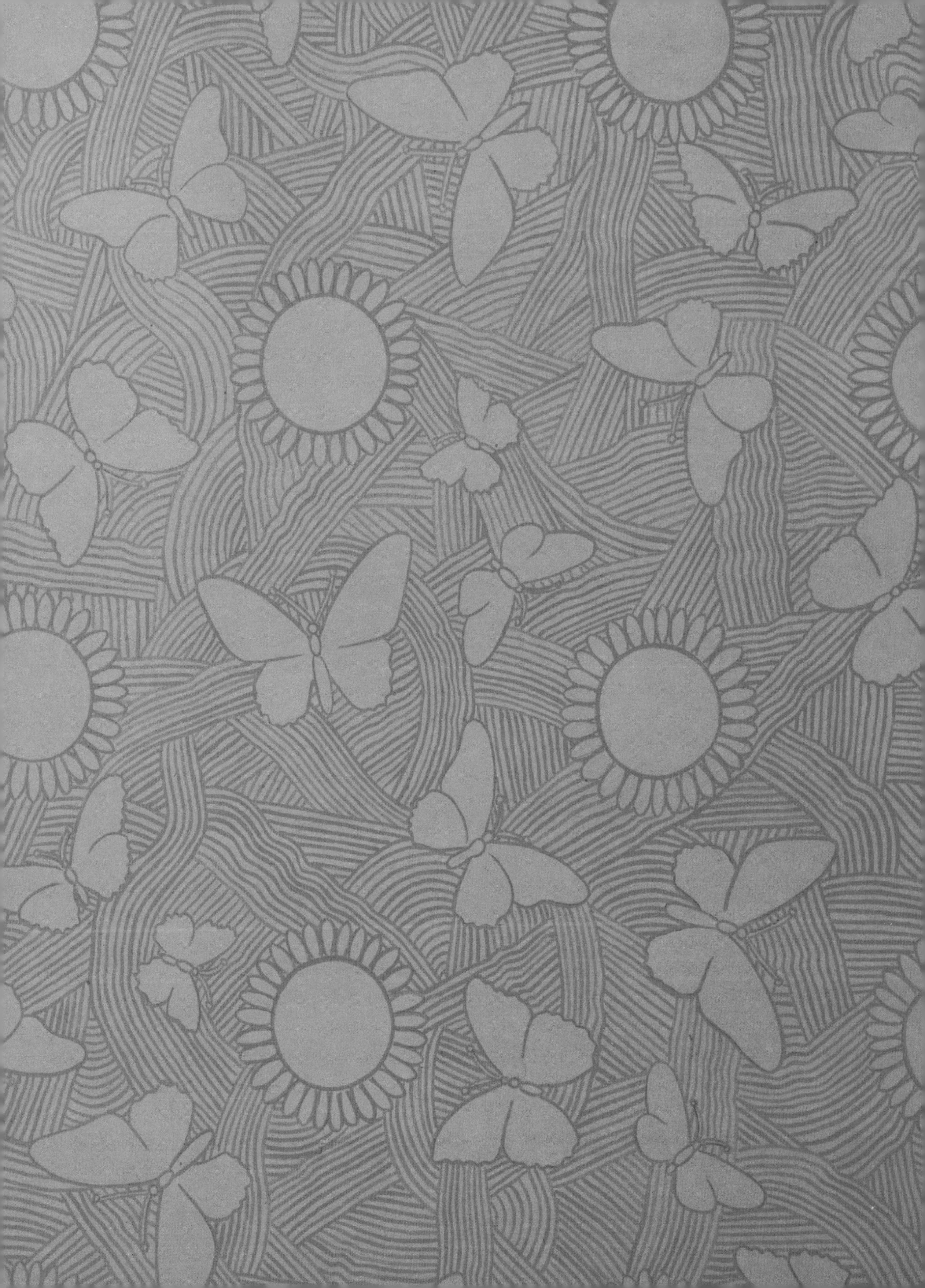